Evan Evans

Some Specimens of the Poetry of the Antient Welsh Bards

Evan Evans

Some Specimens of the Poetry of the Antient Welsh Bards

ISBN/EAN: 9783337329716

Printed in Europe, USA, Canada, Australia, Japan

Cover: Foto ©Andreas Hilbeck / pixelio.de

More available books at **www.hansebooks.com**

SOME

SPECIMENS

OF THE

POETRY

OF THE

ANTIENT WELSH BARDS.

TRANSLATED INTO ENGLISH,

WITH

Explanatory NOTES on the HISTORICAL PASSAGES,

And a fhort Account of MEN and PLACES mentioned by the BARDS,

In order to give the Curious fome Idea of the Tafte and Sentiments of our Anceftors, and their Manner of Writing.

By the Revᵈ Mr. EVAN EVANS,
Curate of LLENVAIR TALYHAERN in DENBIGHSHIRE.

" Vos quoque, qui fortes animas belloque peremptas
" Laudibus in longum, Vates, dimittitis ævum,
" Plurima fecuri fudiftis carmina Bardi."
                                    LUCANUS.

———— " Si quid mea carmina poffunt
" Aonio ftatuam fublimes vertice Bardos,
" Bardos Pieridum cultores atque canentis
" Phœbi delicias, quibus eft data cura perennis
" Dicere nobilium clariffima faċta virorum,
" Aureaque excelfam famam fuper aftra locare."
                        LELANDUS in Affertione Arturii.

LONDON:

Printed for R. and J. DODSLEY in PALL-MALL.

M.DCC.LXIV.

TO

SIR ROGER MOSTYN,

OF

MOSTYN AND GLODDAITH, BART.

Reprefentative of the County, Lord Lieutenant, and Lieutenant
Colonel of the Militia of FLINTSHIRE.

SIR,

I HOPE you will pardon my prefumption in prefixing your
name to the following fmall collection of Britifh poems, to
which you have a juft claim, as being lineally defcended from thofe
heroes they celebrate, and retain in an eminent manner the worth
and generous principles of your renowned anceftors. The Britifh
Bards were received by the nobility and gentry with diftinguifhed
marks of efteem, in every part of Wales, and particularly at Gloddaith
and Moftyn, where their works are ftill preferved in your curious
libraries. I hope, therefore, an attempt to give the public a fmall
fpecimen of their works will not fail of your approbation, which the
editor flatters himfelf with, from the generous manner with which
you treated him, particularly by lending him fome of your valuable
books and manufcripts.

THAT

THAT you may long continue to be an ornament to your country, and a pattern of virtuous actions, and a generous patron of learning, is the fincere wifh, of,

SIR,

Your obliged

Humble Servant,

EVAN EVANS.

The following curious Commiſſion publiſhed and inſerted in ſome of the Copies of Dr. Brown's *Diſſertation on the Union, &c. of Poetry and Muſic, and communicated from a Manuſcript Copy in my Poſſeſſion, having ſo near a Relation to the Family of the noble Patron of theſe Poems, I thought it right to reprint it on this Occaſion.*

" By the QUEEN,

"ELIZABETH, by the Grace of GOD, of England, France, and " Ireland, Queen, Defender of the Faith, &c. To our " truſty and right well beloved beloved Sir Richard Bulkely, Knight, " Sir Rees Griffith, Knight, Ellis Price, Eſq. Dr. in Civil Law, " and one of our Council in the Marcheſſe of Wales, William " Moſtyn, Jeuen Lloyd of Yale, John Saliſbury of Rhug, Rice " Thomas, Maurice Wynne, William Lewis, Pierce Moſtyn, Owen " John ap Howel Fichan, John William ap John, John Lewis " Owen, Morris Griffith, Symmd Thelwat, John Griffith, Ellis ap " William Lloyd, Robert Puleſton, Harri ap Harri, William Glynn, " and Rees Hughes, Eſqrs. and to every of them Greeting."

" WHEREAS it is come to the Knowledge of the Lord Preſident, " and other our Council in our Marcheſſe of Wales, that vagrant and " idle Perſons naming themſelves *Minſtrels, Rythmers,* and *Bards,* are " lately grown into ſuch *intolerable Multitude* within the Principality " of North Wales, that not only Gentlemen and others by their " *ſhameleſs Diſorders* are oftentimes diſquieted in their Habitations, " but alſo the *expert Minſtrels* and *Muſicians* in *Tonge* and *Cunynge* " thereby much diſcouraged to travaile in the Exerciſe and Practiſe " of their Knowledg, and alſo not a little hindred *(of)* Livings and " Preferment; the Reformation whereof, and the putting theſe

5   " People

" People in Order, the said Lord President and Council have thought
" very necessary: And knowing you to be Men of both Wisdom
" and upright Dealing, and also of Experience and good Knwledg
" in the Scyence, have appointed and authorized You to be Commis-
" sioners for that Purpose: And forasmuch as our said Council, of
" late travailing in some Part of the said Principality, had perfect Un-
" derstanding by credible Report, that the accustomed Place for the
" Execution of the like Commission hath been heretofore at Cayroes
" in our County of Flynt, and that William Mostyn, Esq. and his
" Ancestors have had the Gift and bestowing of the *Sylver Harp* ap-
" pertaining to the *Chief* of *that Faculty*, and that a *Year's Warning*
" (at least) hath been accustomed to be given of the *Assembly* and
" Execution of the like Commission; Our said Council have therefore
" appointed the Execution of this Commission to be at the said Town
" of Cayroes, the Monday next after the Feast of the Blessed Trinity
" which shall be in the Year of our Lord 1568. And therefore we
" require and command You by the Authority of these Presents, not
" only to cause *open Proclamation* to be made in all *Fairs, Market-*
" *Towns*, and other *Places of Assembly* within our Counties of Aglere,
" Carnarvon, Meryonydd, Denbigh and Flynt, that all and every
" Person and Persons that intend to *maintain* their *Living* by name
" or Colour of *Minstrels, Rythmers*, or *Bards*, within the Talaith of
" Aberffraw, comprehending the said five Shires, shall be and appear
" before You the said Day and Place to *shew* their *Learnings* accord-
" ingly: But also, that You, twenty, nineteen, eighteen, seventeen,
" sixteen, fifteen, fourteen, thirteen, twelve, eleven, ten, nine, eight,
" seven, or six of you, whereof You the said Sir Richard Bulkely,
" Sir Rees Griffith, Ellis Price, and William Mostyn Esqs. or three
" or two of you, to be of the number; to repair to the said Place the
" Days aforesaid, and calling to you such *expert Men* in the said *Fa-*
                                                                    " *culty*

" *culty* of the *Welſh Muſick* as to You ſhall be thought convenient, to
" proceed to the Execution of the Premiſes, and to admit ſuch and
" ſo many, as by your Wiſdoms and Knowledges you ſhall find
" *worthy*, into and under the *Degrees* heretofore *(in Uſe)* in ſembla-
" ble Sort to *uſe, exerciſe*, and *follow* the *Sciences* and *Faculties* of their
" *Profeſſions*, in ſuch decent Order as ſhall appertain to each of their
" Degrees, and as your Diſcretions and Wiſdoms ſhall preſcribe unto
" them: Giving ſtreight Monition and Commandment in our Name
" and on our Behalf to the reſt not worthy, that they return to ſome
" honeſt Labour, and due Exerciſe, ſuch as they be moſt apt unto
" for Maintenance of their Living, upon Pain to be taken as ſturdy
" and idle Vagabonds, and to be uſed according to the Laws and
" Statutes provided in that Behalf; letting You with our ſaid Coun-
" cil look for Advertiſement, by Certificate at your Hands, of your
" Doings in the Execution of the ſaid Premiſes; foreſeeing in any
" wiſe, that upon the ſaid Aſſembly the Peace and good Order be
" obſerved and kept accordingly; aſcertaining you that the ſaid
" William Moſtyn hath promiſed to ſee Furniture and Things neceſ-
" ſary provided for that Aſſembly, at the Place aforeſaid."

" Given under our Signet at our City of Cheſter, the twenty
" third of October in the ninth Year of our Reign, 1567."

" Signed
" Her Highneſs's Counſail
" in the Marcheſſe of Wales."

" *N. B.* This Commiſſion was copy'd exactly from the Ori-,
" ginal now at Moſtyn, A. D. 1693: Where the *Silver*
" *Harp* alſo is."

Since

Since this Commiſſion has been in the Preſs, the Author has had an Opportunity to ſee the following Account of what has been done in Conſequence of ſuch a Commiſſion in the tenth Year of the Reign of Queen Elizabeth. *This is tranſlated from the Original in* Welſh.

KNOW all Men, by theſe Preſents, That there is a Congreſs of Bards, and Muſicians, to be held in the Town of Caerwys, in the County of Flint, on the twenty-ſixth Day of May, in the tenth Year of the Reign of her Majeſty Queen Elizabeth, before Ellis Price, Eſquire, Doctor of the Civil Law, and one of her Majeſty's Council in the Marches of Wales, and before William Moſtyn, Peres Moſtyn, Owen John ap Hywel Vaughan, John William ap John, John Lewis Owen, Morris Griffith, Simon Thelwat, John Griffith Serjeant, Robert Puleſdon, Evan Lloyd of Jâl, and William Glyn, Eſquires.

AND that we the ſaid Commiſſioners, by virtue of the ſaid Commiſſion, being her Majeſty's Council, do give and grant to Simwnt Vychan, Bard, the degree of Pencerdd ; and do order that Perſons receive and hoſpitably entertain him in all Places fit for him to go and come to receive his Perquiſites according to the Princely Statutes in that Caſe made and provided. Given under our Hands, in the Year 1568.

PREFACE.

PREFACE.

A S there is a natural curiosity in most people to be brought acquainted with the works of men, whose names have been conveyed down to us with applause from very early antiquity; I have been induced to think, that a translation of some of the Welsh Bards would be no unacceptable present to the public. It is true, they lived in times when all Europe was enveloped with the dark cloud of bigotry and ignorance; yet, even under these disadvantageous circumstances, a late instance may convince us, that poetry shone forth with a light, that seems astonishing to many readers. They who have perused the works of Ossian, as translated by Mr. Macpherson, will, I believe, be of my opinion.

I MEAN not to set the following poems in competition with those just mentioned; nor did the success which they have met with from the world, put me upon this undertaking. It was first thought of, and encouraged some years before the name of Ossian was known in England. I had long been convinced, that no nation in Europe possesses greater remains of antient and genuine

B   pieces

pieces of this kind than the Welſh ; and therefore was inclined, in honour to my country, to give a ſpecimen of them in the Engliſh language.

As to the genuineneſs of theſe poems, I think there can be no doubt; but though we may vie with the Scottiſh nation in this particular, yet there is another point, in which we muſt yield to them undoubtedly. The language of their oldeſt poets, it ſeems, is ſtill perfectly intelligible, which is by no means our caſe.

The works of Taliefin, Lywarch Hên, Aneurin Gwawd-rydd, Myrddin Wyllt, Avan Verddig, who all flouriſhed about the year 560, a conſiderable time after Oſſian, are hardly un-derſtood by the beſt critics and antiquarians in Wales, though our language has not undergone more changes than the Erſe. Nay, the Bards that wrote a long while after, from the time of Wil-liam the Conqueror to the death of prince Llewelyn, are not ſo eaſy to be underſtood ; but that whoever goes about to tranſlate them, will find numerous obſolete words, not to be found in any Dictionary or Gloſſary, either in print or manuſcript.

What this difference is owing to, I leave to be determined by others, who are better acquainted, than I am, with ſuch circum-ſtances of the Scottiſh Highlands, as might prove more favour-able towards keeping up the perfect knowledge of their language for ſo many generations. But, be that as it may, it is not my in-tent to enter into the diſpute, which has ariſen in relation to the antiquity of Oſſian's poems. My concern is only about the opinion the world may entertain of the intrinſic value of thoſe which I offer. They ſeem to me, though not ſo methodical and regular

in

in their compofition as many poems of other nations, yet not to be wanting in poetical merit; and if I am not totally deceived in my judgment, I fhall have no reafon to repent of the pains I have taken to draw them out of that ftate of obfcurity, in which they have hitherto been buried, and in which they run great rifque of mouldering away.

It might perhaps be expected, that I fhould fay fomething of the Bards in general on this occafion; but as I have treated that fubject in my Latin Differtation, which I fhall annex to thefe tranflations, it will be fufficient to obferve here, that the ufual fubjects of their poems were the brave feats of their warriors in the field, their hofpitality and generofity with other commendable qualities in domeftic life, and elegies upon their great men, which were fung to the harp at their feafts, before a numerous audience of their friends and relations. This is the account that the Greek and Roman writers have given of them, as I have fhewn at large in the above-mentioned treatife, which I intend to publifh.

The following poems, from among many others of greater length, and of equal merit, were taken from a manufcript of the learned Dr. Davies, author of the Dictionary, which he had tranfcribed from an antient vellum MS. which was wrote, partly in Edward the fecond and third's time, and partly in Henry the fifth's, containing the works of all the Bards from the Conqueft to the death of Llewelyn, the laft prince of the Britifh line. This is a noble treafure, and very rare to be met with; for Edward the firft ordered all our Bards, and their works, to be deftroyed, as is attefted by Sir John Wynne of Gwydir, in the hiftory he compiled of his anceftors at Carnarvon. What remained of their works were conveyed in his

time

time to the Exchequer, where he complains they lay in great confusion, when he had occasion to consult them.

As to the translation, I have endeavoured to render the sense of the Bards faithfully, without confining myself to too servile a version; nor have I, on the other hand, taken liberty to wander much from the originals; unless where I saw it absolutely necessary, on account of the different phraseology and idiom of language.

If this small collection has the good fortune to merit the attention of the public, I may, in some future time, if God permit me life and health, proceed to translate other select pieces from the same manuscript. The poems, in the original, have great merit; and if there is none in the translation of this specimen, it must be owing intirely to my inability to do the Bards justice. I am not the only person who admires them: Men of the greatest sense and learning in Wales do the same.

It must be owned, that it is an arduous task to bring them to make any tolerable figure in a profe translation; but those who have any candor, will make allowances. What was said of poetry in general by one of the wits, that *it is but Profe run mad*, may very justly be applied to our Bards in particular: For there are not such extravagant flights in any poetic compositions, except it be in the Eastern, to which, as far as I can judge by the few tranflated specimens I have seen, they bear a great resemblance.

I have added a few Notes, to illustrate some historical facts alluded to in the poems, and a short account of each poem, and

the

the occasion it was written upon, as far as it could be traced from our ancient manuscripts.

I HAVE been obliged to leave blanks in some places, where I did not understand the meaning in the original, as I had but one copy by me, which might be faulty. When I have an opportunity to collate it with other copies, I may clear these obscure passages.

I.

A POEM *composed by Owain Cyveiliog, prince of Powys, entitled by him* HIRLAS, *from a large drinking horn so called, used at feasts in his palace. He was driven out of his country by Owain Gwynedd, prince of North-wales, and Rhys-ap-Griffith-ap-Rhys-ap-Tewdwr, prince of South-wales, A. D.* 1167, *and recovered it, by the help of the Normans and English, under Henry the second. He flourished about A. D.* 1160, *in the time of Owain Gwynedd and his son David. This poem was composed on account of a battle fought with the English at Maelor, which is a part of the counties of Denbigh and Flint, according to the modern division.*

WHEN the dawn arose, the shout was given; the enemy gave an ominous presage; our men were stained with blood, after a hard contest; and the borders of Maelor Drefred were beheld with wonder and astonishment. Strangers have I driven away undaunted from the field with bloody arms. He that provokes the brave man, ought to dread his resentment.

FILL, Cup-bearer, fill with alacrity the horn of Rhys, in the generous prince's hall; for Owen's hall was ever supported by spoils taken from the enemy; and in it thou hearest of the relief of thousands. There the gates are ever open.

O CUP-

O Cup-bearer, who, with patience, mindeft thy duty, forfake us not; fetch the horn, that we may drink together, whofe glofs is like the wave of the fea; whofe green handles fhew the fkill of the artift, and are tipped with gold. Bring the beft meath, and put it in Gwgan Draws's hand, for the noble feats which he hath atchieved: The offspring of Gronwy, who valiantly fought in the midft of dangers; a race of heroes for worthy acts renowned: And men, who, in every hardfhip they undergo, deferve a reward; who are in the battle foremoft: The guardians of Sabrina. Their friends exult, when they hear their voice. The feftal fhout will ceafe when they are gone.

Fill thou the yellow-tipped horn, badge of honour and mirth, full of frothing meath; and if thou art defirous to have thy life prolonged to the year's end, ftop not the reward due to his virtue; for it is unjuft; and bring it to Griffith, with the crimfon lance. Bring wine in the tranfparent horn; for he is the guardian of * Arwyftii, the defence of its borders; a dragon of Owain the generous, whofe defcent is from Cynvyn; a dragon he was from the beginning, that never was terrified in the battle; his brave actions fhall follow him. The warriors went to purchafe renown, flufhed with liquor, and armed like Edwin; they paid for their mead, like † Belyn's men, in the days of yore. And as long as men exift, their valour fhall be the common theme of Bards.

Fill thou the horn; for it is my inclination, that we may converfe in mirth and feftivity with our brave general; put it in the hand

---

* Arwyftli, the name of one of the cantreds of Powys.

† Belyn, a great man from Lleyn in Carnarvonfhire, mentioned in the Triades, and is faid there to have fought with Edwin, king of the Northumbrians, in Bryn Cenau in Rhos, in the County of Denbigh; probably he was one of Cadwallon's generals; it is well known, and confeffed by Beda himfelf, that That prince was a terrible fcourge to the Saxons.

of

of the worthy Ednyfed, with his spear broken to pieces, and his shield pierced through. Like the bursting of a hurricane upon the smooth sea . . . . in the conflict of battle, they would soon break in pieces the sides of a golden-bordered shield: Their lances were besmeared with gore, after piercing the heads of their enemies; they were vigorous and active in the defence of delightful [a] Garthan. Heard ye in Maelor the noise of war, the horrid din of arms, their furious onset, loud as in the battle of [b] Bangor, where fire flashed out of their spears? There two princes engaged, when the carousing of Morach Vorvran [c] happened.

FILL thou the horn; for it is my delight, in the place where the defenders of our country drink mead, and give it to Selyf the

[a] Garthan, the name of a fort or castle somewhere near the Severn.

[b] This was the famous battle of Bangor-is-y-coed in Flintshire, after the murder of the monks, at the instigation of Austin, the first converter of the Saxons to Christianity. This is the account Humphrey Lloyd gives of that affair: " Ille vero [Augustinus S.] ob hanc contumeliam, & quod archiepiscopo Cantuariæ a se constituto, & quod cum Romana ecclesia in quibusdam non convenirent, Anglorum odium ita in eos concivit, ut paulo post (ut dixi) ab Ethelfredo, Ethelberti, Cantiæ regis, ob Augustino incitati, opera & auxiliis, monachi pacem petentes, crudeliter occisi; & postea Britanni duce Brochwelo Powisiæ Rege, victi sunt, donec tandem Bletrusii Cornaviæ ducis, Cadvanni Northwalliæ, Mereduci Suthwalliæ regum copiis adjuti, & Dunoti abbatis viri doctissimi concione animati, quique jussit (ut nostri annales referunt) ut unusquisque terram oscularetur, in memoriam communionis corporis Dominici, aquamque ex Deva fluvio manu haustam biberet, in memoriam sacratissimi sanguinis Christi pro eis effusi, & ita communicati, memorabili prœlio Saxones, occisis (ut Huntingtonensis refert) ex eis MLXVI. Cadvanumque in civitate Legionis regem creavere." Britan. Descript. Commentariolum, p. 90, & 91, Moses Williams's Edition. This battle is called in our annals sometimes Gwaith Caerlleon, that is, the battle of Chester, and is said to have been fought, A. D. 633.

[c] We have no account at present, that I know of, who this Morach Vorvran was, nor the occasion of his joy and festivity, alluded to in this poem; probably it was upon the defeat of the Saxons at Bangor y Gwygyr.

C   fearless,

fearlefs, the defence of [d] Gwygyr; woe to the wretch that offends him, eagle-hearted heroe: And to the fon of Madoc, the famous and generous Tudur, like a wolf when he feizes his prey, is his af- fault in the onfet. Two heroes, who were fage in their counfels, but active in the field, the two fons of Ynyr, who, on the day of battle, were ready for the attack, heedlefs of danger, famous for their ex- ploits; their affault was like that of ftrong lions, and they pierced their enemies like brave warriors, they were lords of the battle, and rufhed foremoft with their crimfon lances; the weight of their attack was not to be withftood; their fhields were broke afunder with much force, as the high-founding wind on the beach of the green fea, and the encroaching of the furious waves on the coaft of [e] Tal- garth.

FILL, Cup-bearer, as thou regardeft thy life; fill the horn, badge of honour at feafts, the [f] hirlas drinking-horn, which is a token of diftinction, whofe tip is adorned with filver, and it's cover of the fame metal; and bring it to Tudur, the eagle of battles, filled with the beft wine; and if thou doft not bring us the beft of all, thy head fhall fly off: Give it in the hand of Morciddig, encourager of fongs, whofe praife in battle is celebrated; they were brethren of a diftant clime, of an undaunted heart, and their valour was obfervable in their countenance. Can I forget their fervices? . . . . . Impetuous warriors, wolves of the battle, their lances are befmeared with gore; they were the heroes of the chief of [g] Mochnant, in the re- gion of Powys. Their honour was foon purchafed by them both; they feized every occafion to defend their country, in the time of

---

[d] The name of a place, but where fitu- ated, I know not.

[e] Talgarth, the name of many places in Wales; but this muft be fomewhere near the fea.

[f] Hirlas, the epithet of the horn, from hir, long; and glas, blue, or azure.

[g] Mochnannwys, in the original, he calls himfelf prince of the Mochnannwys, or inhabitants of Mochnant.

need,

need, with their bloody arms, and they kept their borders from ho-
ftile invafion. Their lot is praife ; It is like a mournful elegy to me
to lofe them both ! O Chrift! how penfive am I for the lofs of
Moreiddig, which is irreparable.

Po u r thou out the horn, though they defire it not, the drinking
horn, hirlas, with chearfulnefs, and deliver it into the hand of Morgant, one who deferves to be celebrated with diftinguifhed praife. It
was like poifon to me, to be deprived of him, and that he was
pierced - - - - - - by the keen fword.

Po u r, Cup-bearer, from a filver veffel, an honourable gift, badge
of diftinction. On the large plains of [h] Gweftun I have feen a mi-
racle ; to ftop the impetuofity of Gronwy, was more than a tafk
for an hundred men. The warriors pointed their lances, courted
the battle, and were profufe of life ; they met their enemies in the
conflict, and their chieftain was confumed by fire near the furges of
the fea [i]. They refcued a noble prifoner, Meurig the fon of Griffith,
of renowned valour ; they were all of them covered with blood
when they returned, and the high hills and the dales enjoyed the
fun equally [k].

Po u r the horn to the warriors, Owain's noble heroes, who were
equally active and brave. They affembled in that renowned place,

---

[h] Gweftun, the name of a place fomewhere in Powys.

[i] By this circumftance, it feems, they
refcued the prifoner from fome maritime

town.

[k] Sun equally, that is, at noon day,
which added much to the merit of the
action.

where

where the shining steel glittered.   Madoc and Meilir were men accustomed to violence, and maintained each other in the injuries they
did to their enemies; they were the shields of our army, and the
teachers of warlike attack.   Hear ye, by drinking mead, how the
lord of Cattraeth went with his warriors in defence of his just
cause, the guards of [1] Mynyddawc about their distinguished chief.
They have been celebrated for their bravery, and their speedy march.
But nobody has ever performed so noble an exploit as my warriors, in
the tough land of Maelor, in rescuing the captive.

POUR   out, Cup-bearer, sweet and well-strained   mead, (the
thrust of the spear is red in the time of need)   from the horns of
wild oxen, covered with gold, for the honour, and the reward of the
souls of those departed heroes.   Of the numerous cares that surround
princes, no one is conscious here but God and myself.   The man
who neither gives nor takes quarter, and cannot be forced by his
enemies to abide to his word, Daniel the valiant and beautiful:
O Cup-bearer, great is the task to entreat him; his men will not
cease dealing death around them, till he is mollified.   Cup-bearer,
our shares of mead are to be given us equally before the bright
shining tapers.   Cup-bearer, hadst thou seen the action in the land

---

[1] The guards of Mynyddaw Eiddin,
or of Edinborough, in the battle of Cattraeth, which is celebrated by Aneurin
Gwawdrydd, in his heroic poem entitled the Gododin.   Mynyddawc was a
prince of the North, he is mentioned in
the Triades of Britain; and his guards,
who were famous for their loyalty and
bravery, were reckoned among the three
noble guards of the kingdom of Britain; the other two being the guards,
or, as the word Gosgordd may be tranflated, the clans of Melyn the son of
Cynvelyn, and the guards of Drywon
the son of Nudd, in the battle of Rhodwydd Arderydd,

of

of ᵐ Llidwm, the men whom I honour have but what is their juſt reward.   Cup-bearer, hacſt thou ſeen the armed chiefs, encompaſſing
Owain, who were his ſhield againſt the violence of his foes, when
ⁿ Cawres was invaded with great fury.   Cup-bearer, ſlight not my
commands: May we all be admitted into Paradiſe by the King of
kings; and long may the liberty and happineſs of my heroes continue, where the truth is to be diſcerned diſtinctly.

ᵐ Llidwm, the name of a place ſomewhere in Maelor.

ⁿ I do not recollect what country this
place is in.

II. A

II.

A   P   O   E   M

To [a] Myfanwy Fechan of [b] Caftell Dinas Bran, compofed by [c] Howel-ap-Einion Lygliw, a Bard who flourifhed about A. D. 1390.

I AM without fpirit, O thou that haft enchanted me, as [d] Creirwy inchanted [e] Garwy. In whatever part of the world I am, I lament my abfence from the marble caftle of Myfanwy. Love is the heavieft burden, O thou that fhineft like the heavens, and a greater punifhment cannot be inflicted than thy difpleafure, O beautiful Myfanwy. I who am plunged deeper and deeper in love, can expect no other eafe, O gentle fair Myfanwy with the jet eyebrows, than to lofe my life upon thy account. I fung in golden verfe thy praifes, O Myfanwy; this is the happinefs of thy lover,

[a] I cannot recollect who Myfanwy Fechan, the fubject of the poem, is, but guefs her to be defcended from the princes of Powys.

[b] Caftell Dinas Bran, or Bran's Caftle, is fituated on a high hill near Llangollen in Denbighfhire. Mr. Humphrey Llwyd, the Antiquarian, thinks it took its name from Brennus; but Llwyd of the Mufeum, more probably, from Bran, the name of a river that runs thereabout. Bran fignifies a crow, and is the name of feveral rivers in Wales. I fuppofe on account of their black ftreams iffuing from turfaries. There are ftill remains of the ruins of this caftle.

[c] Howel-ap-Einion Lygliw was a man of note in his time, and a celebrated Bard. Dr. Davies thinks he was uncle to Gruffudd Llwyd-ap-Dafydd-ap-Einion Lygliw, another famous bard, who flourifhed, A. D. 1400.

[d] Creirwy, a lady of great beauty often mentioned by the bards.

[e] Garwy, one of king Arthur's knights.

but

but the happiness is a misfortune. The well-fed steed carried me pensive like [f] Trystan, and great was his speed to reach the golden summit of Bran. Daily I turn my eyes, and see thee, O thou that shinest like the waves of [g] Cafwennan. Charming sight to gaze on thee in the spacious royal palace of Bran. I have rode hard, mounted on a fine high-bred steed, upon thy account, O thou with the countenance of cherry-flower bloom. The speed was with eagerness, and the strong long-ham'd steed of [h] Alban reached the summit of the highland of Bran. I have composed, with great study and pains, thy praise, O thou that shinest like the new-fallen snow on the brow of [i] Aran. O thou beautiful flower descended from [k] Trefor. Hear my sorrowful complaint. I am wounded, and the great love I bear thee will not suffer me to sleep, unless thou givest me a kind answer. I, thy pensive Bard, am in as woeful plight as [l] Rhun by thy palace, beautiful maid. I recite, without either flattery or guile, thy praise, O thou that shinest like the meridian sun, with thy stately steps. Shouldst thou, who art the luminary of many countries, demand my two eyes, I would part with them on thy account, such is the pain I suffer. They pain me while I look on the glossy walls of thy fine habitation, and see thee beautiful as the morning sun. I have meditated thy praise, and made all countries resound with it, and every finger was pleased in chanting it. So affecting are the subjects of my mournful tale, O Myfanwy [m], that lookest like

---

[f] Tryftan - ap - Tallwch, another of king Arthur's knights.

[g] Cafwennan, the name of one of king Arthur's ships, which was wrecked in a place denominated from her Goffrydau Cafwennan.

[h] Alban, Scotland. It seems the Bard rode upon a Scotch steed.

[i] Aran, the name of two high mountains in Merionethshire.

[k] Some of the Trefor - family (and perhaps descendents) now live near Castell Dinas Bran.

[l] Rhen, son of Maelgwn Gwynedd king of Britain, A. D. 570. I do not remember the story alluded to here by the Bard.

[m] I suppose Myfanwy Fechan was descended from Tudur Trefor earl of Hereford, of one side. The worthy family of the Moftyns of Moftyn and Gloddaith, are descended from Tudur Trefor.

flakes

flakes of driven fnow.   My loving heart finks with grief without
thy fupport, O thou that haft the whitenefs of the curling waves.
Heaven has decreed, that I fhould fuffer tormenting pain, and wifdom
and reafon were given in vain to guard againft love.   When I faw thy
fine fhape in fcarlet robes, thou daughter of a generous chief, I was
fo affected, that life and death were equal to me.   I funk away, and
fcarce had time to make my confeffion.   Alas! my labour in celebrating thy praifes, O thou that fhineft like the fine fpider's webs on
the grafs in a fummer's day, is vain.   It would be a hard tafk for any
man to guefs how great my pain is.   It is fo afflicting, thou bright
luminary of maids, that my colour is gone.   I know that this pain
will avail me nothing towards obtaining thy love, O thou whofe
countenance is as bright as the flowers of the haw-thorn.   O how
well didft thou fucceed in making me to languifh, and defpair.   For
heaven's fake, pity my diftreffed condition, and foften the pennance of
thy Bard.   I am a Bard, who, though wounded by thee, fing thy
praifes in well-founding verfe, thou gentle maid of flender fhape,
who hindereft me to fleep by thy charms.   I bring thy praifes,
bright maid, to thy neat palace at ⁿ Dinbrain; many are the fongs
that I rehearfe to celebrate thy beautiful form.

ⁿ Dinbrain, the fame as Dinas Bran.

A N

III.

A N O D E

Of David Benvras to Llewelyn the Great, Prince of Wales, A. D. 1240.

HE who created the glorious sun, and that cold pale luminary the moon, grant that I attain the heights of poetry, and be inspired with the genius of [a] Myrddin; that I may extol the praise of of heroes, like [b] Aneurin, in the day he sung his celebrated Gododin; that I may set forth the happiness of the inhabitants of Venedotia, the noble and prosperous prince of Gwynedd, the stay and prop of his fair and pleasant country. He is manly and heroic in the battle, his fame overspreadeth the country about the mountain of [c] Breiddin. Since God created the first man, there never was his

---

[b] There were two Myrddins, or Merlins, as they are wrongly written by the English, viz. Myrddin Emrys and Myrddin Wyllt; the last was a noted poet, and there is a poem of his extant, entitled Avallennau, or the Apple-trees.

[b] Aneurin Gwawdrydd Mychdeyrn Beirdd, i. e. Aneurin the monarch of Bards, was a celebrated poet of North Britain. His poem, the Gododin, upon the battle of Cattraeth, is extant; but by reason of it's great antiquity, is not easily understood at this distance of time, being upwards of twelve hundred years old: However, it appeas, from what is understood of it, to have been a very spirited performance.

[c] Craig Vreiddin, is a high hill in Montgomeryshire.

D   equal

equal in the front of battle. Llewelyn the generous, of the race of princes, has ſtruck terror and aſtoniſhment in the heart of kings. When he ſtrove for ſuperiority with Loegria's king, when he was waſting the country of [d] Erbin, his troops were valiant and numerous. Great was the confuſion when the ſhout was given, his ſword was bathed in blood ; proud were his nobles to ſee his army; when they heard the claſhing of ſwords, then was felt the agony of wounds [e] - - - - - - - -
- - - - - - - - - -

Many were the gaſhes in the conflict of war. Great was the confuſion of the Saxons about the ditch of Knocking [f]. The ſword was broke in the hand of the warrior. Heads were covered with wounds, and the flood of human gore guſhed in ſtreams down the knees.

LLEWELYN's empire is wide extended, he is renowned as far as [g] Porth Yſgewin. Conſtahtine was not his equal in undergoing hardſhips. Had I arrived to the height of prophecy, and the great gift of antient poeſy, I could not relate his proweſs in action ; no, [h] Talieſin himſelf was unequal to the taſk. Before he finiſhes his courſe in this world, after he has lived a long life on earth, ere he goes to the deep and bone-beſtrewed grave, ere the green herb grows over

---

[d] I know not where this country is.

[e] Some lines are wanting in the original.

[f] Knocking, I ſupppoſe, is ſomwhere near Offa's ditch.

[g] Porth Yſgewin is near Chepſtow, in Monmouthſhire or Glamorganſhire.

[h] Talieſin Ben Beridd, or the chief of Bards, flouriſhed about the year 560, or thereabout, under Maelgwn Gwynedd king of Britain, called by Gildas Maglocunus. Many of Talieſin's poems are extant, but on account of their great antiquity are very obſcure, as the work of his cotemporaries are. There is a great deal of the Druidical Cabbala intermixed in his works, eſpecially about the tranſmigration of ſouls.

his

his tomb, may he that turned the water into wine, grant that he may have the Almighty's protection ; and that for every fin, with which he hath been ftrained, he may receive remiffion. May Llewelyn, the noble and generous, never be confounded or afhamed when he arrives at that period ; and may he be under the protection of the faints.

IV.

A   P   O   E   M

To Llewelyn the Great, compofed by Einion the Son of Gwgan, about 1244.

I INVOKE the affiftance of the God of Heaven, Chrift our Saviour, whom to neglect is impious. That gift is true which defcendeth f.om above. The gifts that are given me are immortal, to difcern, according to the great apoftle, *what is right and decent*; and, among other grand fubjects, to celebrate my prince, who avoids not the battle nor it's danger; Llewelyn the generous, the maintainer of bards. He is the difpenfer of happinefs to his fubjects, his noble deeds cannot be fufficiently extolled. His fpear flafhes in a hand accuftomed to martial deeds. It kills and puts it's enemies to flight by the palace of Rheidiol [a]. I have feen, and it was my heart's delight, the guards of Lleifion [b] about it's grand buildings; numberlefs troops of warriors mounted on white fteeds. They encompaffed

---

[a] Rheidiol is the name of a large river in Cardiganfhire, and Glafgrug, one of the palaces of the princes of South-wales, is very near it, about a meafured mile from Aberyftwyth, and at prefent the property of the Rev. Mr. William Powel of Nanteos.

[b] Lleifion was one of the palaces of the princes of Powys, corruptly now called Llyfin; and the park about it is called Llyfin-park, the patrimony of lord Powys.

our eagle: Llewelyn the magnanimous hero, whofe armour gliftered; the maintainer of his rights.   He defended the border of Powys, a country renowned for it's bravery, he defended it's fteep paffes, and fupported the privileges of it's prince.   Obftinate was his refiftance to the treacherous Englifh.   In Rhuddlan he was like the ruddy fire flaming with deftructive light   There have I feen Llewelyn the brave gaining immortal glory.   I have feen him gallantly ploughing the waves of Deva, when the tide was at it's height.   I have feen him furious in the conflict of Chefter, where he doubly repays his enemies the injuries he fuffered from them.   It is but juft that he fhould enjoy the praife due to his valour.   I will extol thee, and the tafk is delightful.   Thou art like the eagle amongft the nobles of Britain. Thy form is majeftic and terrible, when thou purfueft thy foes. When thou invadeft thy enemies, where Owain thy predeceffor invaded them in former times; full proud was thy heart in dividing the fpoils, it happened as in the battles of Kulwydd and Llwyvein[c]. Thy beautiful fteeds were fatigued with the labour of the day, where the troops wallowed in gore, and were thrown in confufion.   The bow was full bent before the mangled corfe, the fpear aimed at the breaft, in the country of Eurgain[d].   The army at Offa's Dike panted for glory, the troops of Venedotia, and the men of London, were as the alternate motion of the waves on the fea-fhore, where the fea-mew fcreams; great was our happinefs to put the Normans to fear and confternation.   Llewelyn the terrible with his brave warriors effected it; the prince of glorious and happy Mona.   He is it's ornament and diftinguifhed chief.

[c] The battle of Llwyvein was fought by Urien Reged and his fon Owain, againft Ida king of the Nortnumbrians. It is celebrated by Taliefin in a poem, entitled Gwaith Argoed Llwyvein, i. e. the battle of Argoed Llwyvein.

[d] Eurgain, Northop in Flintfhire, fo called from Eurgain, the daughter of Maelgwn Gwynedd.

THE lord of Demetia [e] muftered his troops, and out of envy met his prince in the field. The inhabitants of Stone-walled Carmarthen were hewn to pieces in the conflict. Nor fort, nor caftle, could withftand him : And before the gates the Englifh were trampled under foot. It's chief was fad, the unfheathed fword fhone bright, and hundreds hands were engaged in the onfet at Llanthadian [f]. In [g] Cilgeran they purchafed glory and honour . . . : . . . . In Abér Terior the hovering crows were numberlefs . . . thick were the fpears befmeared with gore. The ravens croaked, they were greedy to fuck the proftrate carcafes. Llewelyn, may fuch fate attend thy foes. Mayeft thou be more profperous than the noble [h] Llywarch with his bloody lance. Thy glory fhall not be obfcured. There is none that exceedeth thee in beftowing gifts on the days of folemnity. In battle thy fword is confpicuous. Wherever thou goeft to war, to whatever diftant clime, glory follows thee from the rifing to the fetting fun. I have a generous and noble prince, the lord of a large territory. He is renowned for his coolnefs and conduct. Whole troops fall before him ; he defendeth his men like an eagle. My prince's brave actions will be celebrated in the

---

[e] Demetia. This expedition of Llewelyn-ap-Iorwerth was againft the Flemings and Normans, of which there is an account in Powel's Hiftory of Wales, p. 277, 278.

[f] Llanhuadein the name of a place in Pembrokefhire.

[g] Cilgeran the name of another place in the fame county, near the river Tievi.

[h] Llywarch-hen, the fon of Elidir Lydnwyn a nobleman of North Britain, and coufin german to Urien Reged king of Cumbria, he was a great warrior, and fought fuccefsful againft the Saxons ; but fortune at laft favouring the Saxons, he was obliged in his old age to retire to Wales. He had twenty-four fons, who wore golden chains, and were all killed in battles againft the Saxons. Llywarch-hen was a noted Bard, his works are extant, wherein he celebrates the noble feats of his fons, and bewails his misfortunes, and the troubles of old age, efpecially in diftrefs.

country

country by Tanad[i]. He is valorous as a lion, who can refift his lance ? He is charitable to the needy, and his relief is not fought in vain. My prince is dreffed in fine purple robes. He is like generous [k] Nudd in beftowing prefent. Like valiant [l] Huail in defying his enemy. He is like [m] Rhydderch in diftributing his gold. Let his praife refound in every country. He poffeffes a large territory and immenfe riches, wherever you turn your eyes. In wealth he is equal to Mordaf; like him he opens his liberal hand to the Bard. He is like warlike [n] Rhun in beftowing his favours. He is the fubject of my meditation. I am to him as an hand or an eye. He is not defcended from a bafe degenerate ftock; and I myfelf am defcended from his father's courtiers. His fury in battle is like lightning when he attacks the foe: His heart glows with ardour in the field like magnanimous Gwriad [p]. His enemies are fcattered as leaves on the fide of hills drove by tempeftuous hurricanes. He is the honourable fupport and owner of Hunydd [q]. He is the grace, the ornament of Arvon [r]. Llewelyn, terror of thy enemy, death iffued out of thy hand in the South. Thou art to us like an anchor in the time of ftorm. Protector of our country, may the fhield of God protect thee. Britain, fearlefs of her enemies, glories in being ruled by

[i] Tanad is the name of a river in Montgomeryfhire, which emptieth itfelf into the Severn.

[k] Nudd Hael, or the Generous, was a nobleman of North Britain remarkable for his liberality.

[l] Huail was a brother of Gildas, the fon of Caw, and a noted warrior. His brother Gildas was the author of the Epiftle De excidio Britanniae.

[m] Rydderch Hael, or the Generous, was another nobleman of the North, noted for his liberality.

[n] Rhun, the fon of Maelgwn Gwinedd king of Britain, a great warrior.

[o] As an hand, &c. i. e. I am as neceffary to him as one of thofe members to the body, to celebrate his martial feats.

[p] Gwriad, is the name of a hero mentioned in the Gododin.

[q] Hunydd, the name of a woman, probably the prince's miftrefs. The Bard had no great affection for Joan the princefs, daughter of king John, becaufe fhe was an Englifhwoman, and not faithful to the prince's bed.

[r] Arvon, the county of Crnarvon, fo called, becaufe fituated oppofite to Mòn, or Anglefea. Arvon, literally Supra Monam, from the particle Ar, fuper, and Mon, Mona.

I

him

him, by a chief who has numerous troops to defend her ; by Llewelyn, who defies his enemies from fhore to fhore. He is the joy of armies, and like a lyon in danger. He is the emperor and fovereign of fea and land. He is a warrior that may be compared to a deluge, to the furge on the beach that covereth the wild falmons. His noife is like the roaring wave that rufheth to the fhore, that can neither be ftopped or appeafed. He puts numerous troops of his enemies to flight like a mighty wind. Warriors crowded about him, zealous to defend his juft caufe ; their fhields fhone bright on their arms. His Bards make the vales refound with his praifes ; the juftice of his caufe, and his bravery in maintaining it, are defervedly celebrated. His valor is the theme of every tongue. The glory of his victories is heard in diftant climes. His men exult about their eagle. To yield or die is the fate of his enemies—They have experienced his force by the fhivering of his lance. In the day of battle no danger can turn him from his purpofe. He is confpicuous above the reft, with a large, ftrong, crimfon lance. He is the honour of his country, great is his generofity, and a fuit is not made to him in vain. Llewelyn is a tender-hearted prince. He can nobly fpread the feaft, yet is he not enervated by luxury. May he that beftowed on us a fhare of his heavenly revelation, grant him the bleffed habitation of the faints above the ftars.

V. A

A PANEGYRIC

Upon Owain Gwynedd, Prince of North Wales, by Gwalchmai, the Son of Melir, in the Year **1157.**

I WILL extol the generous hero defcended from the race of [a] Roderic, the bulwark of his country, a prince eminent for his good qualities, the glory of Britain, Owain the brave and expert in arms, a prince that neither hoardeth nor coveteth riches.——Three fleets arrived, veffels of the main, three powerful fleets of the firft rate, furioufly to attack him on a fudden. One from [b] Iwerddon, the other full of well-armed [c] Lochlynians, making a grand appearance on the floods, the third from the tranfmarine [d] Normans, which was attended with an immenfe, though fuccefslefs toil.

---

[a] Owain Gwynedd, prince of North Wales, was defcended in a direct line from Roderic the Great, prince of all Wales, who divided his principality amongft his three fons.

[b] Iwerddon, the Britifh name of Ireland, hence the Hibernia of the Latins, and 'Ιερη and 'Ιερνια of the Greeks, probably fo called from the Britifh Y Werdd Ynys, i. e. the Green Ifland.

[c] Lochlynians, the Danes, fo called from the Baltic, which our anceftors called Llychlyn. Llychlyn is the name of Denmark and Norway, and all thofe northern regions mentioned in the works of our Bards.

[d] Normans. Mofes Williams in his notes on the Ærae Cambro Britannicae gives the following account of this battle.

The Dragon of Mona's [e] fons were fo brave in action, that there was a great tumult on their furious attack, and before the prince himfelf, there was vaft confufion, havock, conflict, honourable death, bloody battle, horrible confternation, and upon Tal Moelvre a thoufand banners. There was an outrageous [f] carnage, and the rage of fpears, and hafty figns of violent indignation. Blood raifed the tide of the Menai, and the crimfon of human gore ftained the brine. There were glittering cuiraffes, and the agony of gafhing wounds, and the mangled warriors proftrate before the chief, diftinguifhed by his crimfon lance. Lloegria was put into confufion, the conteft and confufion was great, and the glory of our prince's wide-wafting fword fhall be celebrated in an hundred languages to give him his merited praife.

" Normanni, qui in hoc loco Frainc " appellantur, erant copiæ quas Henricus " Secundus in Monam mifit A. D. " MCLVII. duce Madoco filio Mare- " dudii Powifiæ principe. Hi ecclefias " SS. Mariæ et Petri (ut annales noftri " referunt) fpoliavere. Iftæ vero ecclefiæ " in orientali Monæ plaga funt, unde " liquet locum Tal Moelvre dictum ali- " cubi in Mona effe, fortaffe etiam haud " procul ab ecclefiis prædictis : omnes " vero qui navibus egrediebantur a Monæ " incolis interfecti funt." Vide Anna-les a Powelo edictos, p. 206, 207.

It feems by Gwalmach's poem to have been a very large fleet, which came part-ly from Ireland, partly from the Baltic, and the reft from Normandy, to invade the principality. It is plain that it's forces were numerous, as they came from fo many countries ; but [*] it feems they met with a very warm recep-tion, from the prince and his fons ; and that they were glad to fail away as foon as poffible.

[e] Owen Gwynedd had many fons noted for their valour, efpecially Howel, who was born of Finnog an Irifh lady. He was one of his father's generals in his wars againft the Englifh, Flemings, and Normans, in South Wales, and was a noted Bard, as feveral of his poems, now extant, teftify.

[f] It feems that the fleet landed in fome part of the firth of Menai, and that it was a kind of a mixt engagement, fome fight-ing on fhore, others from the fhips. And probably the great flaughter was owing to it's being low water, and that they could not fet fail : otherwife I fee no reafon, why when they were worfted on land, they fhould continue the fight in their fhips. It is very plain that they were in great di-ftrefs, and that there was a great havock made of them, as appears from the re-mainder of this very fpirited poem.

VI. A N

VI.

A N   E L E G Y

To [a] *Neſt, the daughter of Howel by Einion the ſon of Gwalchmai, about the year* 1240.

THE ſpring returns, the trees are in their bloom, and the foreſt in it's beauty, the birds chaunt, the ſea is ſmooth, the gently-riſing tide ſounds hollow, the wind is ſtill. The beſt armour againſt misfortune is prayer. But I cannot hide nor conceal my grief, nor can I be ſtill and ſilent. I have heard the waves raging furiouſly towards the confines of the land of the ſons of [b] Beli. The ſea flowed with force, and conveyed a hoarſe complaining noiſe, on account of a Gentle Maiden. I have paſſed the deep waters of the Teivi [c] with ſlow ſteps. I ſung the praiſe of Neſt ere ſhe died. Thouſands have reſounded her name, like that of Elivri [d]. But now I muſt with a penſive and ſorrowful

---

[a] Who this lady was is not known at preſent.
[b] What country this is I cannot re-collect.

[c] Teivi, the name of a large river in Cardiganſhire.
[d] Elivri, the name of a woman, but who ſhe was, or when ſhe lived, is not clear.

E 2

heart

heart compofe her elegy, a fubject fraught with mifery. The bright luminary of * Cadvan was arrayed in filk, how beautiful did fhe fhine on the banks of ᶠ Dyfynni, how great was her innocence and fimplicity, joined with confummate prudence : fhe was above the bafe arts of diffimulation. Now the ruddy earth covers her in filence. How great was our grief, when fhe was laid in her ftony habitation. The burying of Neft was an irreparable lofs. Her eye was as fharp as the hawk, which argued her defcended from noble anceftors. She added to her native beauty by her goodnefs and virtue. She was the ornament of Venedotia, and her pride. She rewarded the Bard generoufly. Never was pain equal to what I fuffer for her lofs. Oh death, I feel thy fting, thou haft undone me. No man upon earth regretteth her lofs like 'me; but hard fate regardeth not the importunity of prayers, whenever mankind are deftined to undergo it's power. O generous Neft, thou lieft in thy fafe retreat, I am penfive and melancholy like ᵍ Pryderi. I ftore up my forrow in my breaft, and cannot difcharge the heavy burden. The dark, lonefome dreary veil, which covereth thy face, is ever before me, which covereth a face that fhone like the pearly dew on Eryri ʰ. I make my humble petition to the great Creator of heaven and earth, and my petition will not be denied, that he grant, that this beautiful maid, who glittered like pearls, may, through the interceffion of Holy ᶦ Dewi,

---

ᵉ Cadvan is the faint of Towyn Meirionnydd.

ᶠ Dyfvnni, is the name of a river that runs by Towyn.

ᵍ I cannot recollect at prefent who this perfon is, nor the occafion of his grief, though it is mentioned in fome of our manufcripts.

ʰ Eryri Snowdon, called Creigian,

Eryri and Mynydd Eryri, i. e. the rocks and mountains of fnow, from Eiry, which fignifies fnow. As Niph..tes the name of a mountain, from a word of the fame fignification in Greek.

ᶦ Dewi, St. David, a bifhop in the time of king Arthur, and the patron Saint of Wales.

be received to his mercy, that fhe may converfe with the prophets, that fhe may come into the inheritance of the All-wife God, with Mary and the Martyrs. And in her behalf I will prefer my prayer, which will fly to the throne of Heaven. My love and affection knew no bounds. May fhe never fuffer. Saint Peter be her protector. God himfelf will not fuffer her to be an exile from the manfions of blifs. Heaven be her lot.

VII. A

VII.

A P O E M

To Llywelyn ap Jorweth, or Llywelyn the Great;

In which many of his victories are celebrated;

Composed by Llywarch Brydydd y Moch, a Bard, who, according to Mr. Edward Lhwyd of the Musæum's Catalogue of the British writers, flourished about the year 1240; but this poem is certainly of more antient date; for prince Llywelyn died in the year 1240. However that be, the original was taken from Lyfr Coch o Hergeſt, or the Red book of Hergeſt, kept in the Archives of Jeſus College, Oxon. I have no apology to make for the Bards method of beginning or concluding their poems, but that it was their general cuſtom ever ſince the introduction of Chriſtianity to this iſland, which was very early. We have no poems that I know of before that period, but ſome few remains of the Druids in that kind of verſe, called Englyn Milwr. It was the cuſtom of the heathen poets themſelves to begin their poems with an invocation of the Supreme Being. As for inſtance, Theocritus in the beginning of his Idyllium, in praiſe of Ptolemæus Philadelphus,

'Εκ Διὸς ἀρχώμεϑα, χ̩ εἰς Δία λήγέͅε, Μοῖσαι.

But I ſhall not here enter into a critical diſſertation of their merits or defects; my buſineſs, as a translator, being to give as faithful a verſion

4

from

from the original as I possibly could at this distance of time ; when many
of the matters of fact, the manners of the age, and other circumstances,
alluded to in their poems, must remain obscure to those that are best versed
in the records of antiquity.

MAY Christ the Creator and Governor of the hosts of heaven
and earth defend me from all disasters ; may I, through his
assistance, be prudent and discreet ere I come to my narrow habitation in the grave.   Christ, the Son of God, will give me the gift of
song to extol my prince, who giveth the warlike shout with joy.
Christ who hath formed me of the four elements, and hath endowed
me with the deep and wonderful gift of poetry — Llywelyn is the
ruler of Britain and her armour.   He is a lion-like brave prince, un-
moved in action, the son of ᵃ Jorwerth, our strength and true friend,
a descendant of ᵇ Owain the destroyer, whose abilities appeared in
his youth.   He came to be a leader of forces, dressed in blue, neat
and handsome.   In the conflicts of battle, in the clang of arms, he
was an heroic youth.   When ten years old he successfully attacked
his kinsman ᶜ.   In Aber Conwy, ere my prince, the brave Llywelyn,
got his right, he contested with ᵈ David, who was a bloody chief,
like Julius Cæsar.   A chief without blemish, not insulting his foes in
distress, but in war impetuous and fierce, like the points of flaming
fire burning in their rage.   It is a general loss to the Bards, that he

---

ᵃ Jorwerth, surnamed Drwydwr, or with the broken nose, the father of Lly-welyn, was the eldest son of Owain Gwy-nedd, but was not suffered to enjoy his right on an the account of that blemish.

ᵇ Owain Gwynedd, prince of North Wales.

ᶜ Llywelyn was the lawful heir of the principality of North Wales, in right of his father Jorwerth, and accordingly put in his claim for it, and got it from his uncles David and Rodri, when he was very young.

ᵈ David, the son of Owain Gwynedd, who succeeded his father as prince of Wales.

is

is covered with earth. We grieve for him. — ‘ Llywelyn was our prince ere the furious conteſt happened, and the ſpoils were amaſſed with eagerneſs. The purple gore ran over the ſnow-white breaſts of the warriors, and there was an univerſal havock and carnage after the ſhout. The parti-coloured waves flowed over the broken ſpear, and the warriors were ſilent. The briny wave came with force, and another met it mixed with blood, when we went to Porthae-thwy on the ſteeds of the main over the great roaring of the floods. The ſpear raged with relentleſs fury, and the tide of blood ruſhed with force. Our attack was ſudden and fierce. Death diſplayed itſelf in all it's horrors: So that it was a doubt whether any of us ſhould die of old age. Noble troops, in the fatal hour, trampled on the dead like prancing ſteeds. Before Rhodri was brought to ſub-miſſion, the church-yards were like fallow grounds. When Llywe-lyn the ſuccefsful prince overcome by ᶠ Alun with his warriors of the bright arms, ten thouſand were killed, and the crows made a noiſe, and a thouſand were taken priſoners. Llywelyn, though in battle he killed with fury, though he burnt like outrageous fire, yet was mild prince when the mead-horns were diſtributed - - -

he a - - - - he gave generouſly under his waving banners to his numerous Bards gold and ſilver, which he re-gardeth not, and Gaſcony prancing ſteeds, with rich trappings, and and great ſcarlet cloaks, ſhining like the ruddy flame: Warlike, ſtrong, well-made deſtroying ſteeds, with ſtreams of foam iſſuing out of their mouths. He generouſly beſtoweth, like brave Arthur, ſnow-white ſteeds by hundreds, whoſe ſpeed is fleeter than birds.

‘ This battle is not mentioned by any of our hiſtorians. The deſcription is very animated in the original, and very expreſſive of ſuch a ſcene. It was fought near Porth Aethwy. The ſteeds of the main is a poetical expreſſion for ſhips.

ᶠ Alun, the name of a river in Flint-ſhire, where there was a battle fought by Llywelyn againſt the Engliſh.

Thou

Thou that feedest the fowls of the air like [g] Caeawg the hero, the valiant ruler of all Britain, the numerous forces of England tumble and wallow in the field before thee. He bravely atchieved above [h] Deudraeth Dryfan, the feats of the renowned Ogrfani [i]. Men fall silently in the field, and are deprived of the rites of sepulture. Thou haft defeated two numerous armies, one in the banks of Alun of the rich foil, where the Normans were deftroyed, as the adverfaries of Arthur, in the battle of Camlan [k]. The fecond in Arfon, near the fea-fhore - - - - - - And two ruling chiefs, flufhed with fuccefs, encouraged us like lions, and one fuperior to them both, a ftern hero, the ravage of battles, like a man that conquers in all places. Llywelyn with the broken blade of the gilt fword, the wafter of Lloegr, a wolf covered with red, with his warriors about Rhuddlan. His forces carry the ftandard before him waving in the air. Thou art poffeffed of the valour of [l] Cadwallon, the fon of Cadfan. He is for recovering the government of all Britain. He kindly ftretched his hand to us, while his enemies fled to the fea-fhore, to embark to avoid the imminent deftruction, with

[g] Caeawg Cynnorawg, is the name of a hero celebrated by Aneurin Gwawdrydd in the Gododin.

[h] Deudraeth Cryfan, is the name of fome place near the fea, there are many places in Wales called Deudraeth. But where this in particular is fituated I cannot guefs.

[i] Ogrfan Gwr, an antient Britifh prince, cotemporary with king Arthur.

[k] Camlan, the name of a place fomewhere in Cornwal, where the decifive battle between king Arthur, and his treacherous nephew Medrod happened, who had ufurped the fovereignty while he was absent on a foreign expedition. King Arthur, according to our antient hiftorians, flew Medrod with his own hand; but received his death-wound himfelf, and retired to Ynys Afallon or Glaftenbury, where he foon afterwards died. His death was politically concealed, leaft it fhould difpirit the Britons. Hence arofe fo many fabulous ftories about it.

[l] Cadwallon, the fon of Cadfan, is that victorious king of Britain, who was a terrible fcourge to the Saxons. Beda in his ecclefiaftical hiftory calls him tyrannum fævientem, an outrageous tyrant.

F   defpair

defpair in their looks, and no place of refuge remained, and the crimfon lance whizzed dreadfully over their brows. We the Bards of Britain, whom our prince entertaineth on the Firſt of January, fhall every one of us, in our rank and ftation, enjoy mirth and jollity, and receive gold and filver for our reward   -   -   -

-    -   -   -   -   -   -   -   -

-    -   -   -   -   -   -   -

-    -   -   -   -   -   -   -

^m Caer Lleon, the chief of Mon, has brought thee to a low condi-
tion. Llewelyn has wafted thy land, thy men are killed by the fea

-    -   -   -   -   -   -   -   -   -

He has entirely fubdued ⁿ Gwyddgrug, where the Englifh ran away, with a precipitate flight, full of horror and confternation. Thy fields are miferably wafted, thy cloifter, and thy neat houfes, are afhes. The palace of ^o Elfmer was with rage and fury burnt by fire. Ye all now enjoy peace by fubmiting to our prince, for wherever he goeth with his forces, whether it be hill or dale, it is the poffeffion of one fole proprietor. Our lion has brought to Trallwng three armies that will never turn their backs, the refidence of our enemies ever to be abhorred. The numerous Bards receive diverfe favours from him. He took Gwyddgrug. See you who fucceeds in ^p Mochnant when he victorioufly marches through your country. On it's borders the

---

^m Caer Lleon Chefter, fo called, as our hiftorians relate, from Lleon Gawr, or king Lleon, and not from Caftra legionum, as modern writers will have it. Gawr antiently fignified a king, as Benlli Gwr, is called by Nennius, cap. 30, Rex Benlli; but now it fignifies a giant, or a man of an extraordinary ftrength and flature. It is not improbable but that

the Antient Britons chofe fuch for their kings.

ⁿ Gwyddrug Mold, in Flintfhire, fo called from Gwydd high, and Crag a hill. Mold is a corruption of Mons altus.

^o Elfmer, the name of a town in Shrop-fhire.

^p Mochnant is a part of Powys.

enemy

enemy were routed, and the ^q Argoedwys were furiously attacked, and covered with blood. We have two palaces now in our possession. Let ^r Powys see who is the valiant king of her people, whether it argueth prudence to act treacherously. Whether a Norman chief be preferable to a conquering Cymro. We have a prince, consider it, who, though silent about his own merit, putteth Lloegr to flight, and is fully bent to conquer the land that was formerly in the possession of Cadwallon, the son of Cadfan, the son of Jago - - - - - - - -

- - - - - - - - -

A noble lion, the governor of Britain, and her defence. Llywelyn, numerous are thy battles, thou brave prince of the mighty, that puttest the enemy to flight. Mayest thou my friend and benefactor overcome in every hardship. He is a prince with terrible looks who will conquer in foreign countries, as well as in Mon the mother of all Wales. His army has made it's way broad thro' the ocean, and filled the hills, promontories and dales. The blood flowed about their feet when the maimed warriors fought. In the battle of ^s Coed Anea, thou, supporter of Bards, didst overthrow thy enemies. The other hard battle was fought at ^t Dygen Ddyfnant, where thousands behaved themselves with manly valour. The next contest, where noble feats were achieved, was on the hill of ^u Bryn Yr Erw, where they saw

^q Argoedwys, the men of Powys, from Ar above, Coed wood. The Powysians are called, by Llywarch, Hen Gwr Argoed. As Gwyr Argoed cried am porthant, i. e. I was ever maintained by the men of Argoed.

^r The princes of Powys adhered to the kings of England, and the Lords Marchers, against their natural prince, to whom they were to pay homage and obedience, according to the division made by Rhodri Mawr, as appears from the Welsh history.

^s Coed Anea, the name of a place, but where situated I cannot guess, where a battle was fought.

^t Dygen Ddyfnant, another place whose situation I am ignorant of, where another battle was fought.

^u Bryn Yr Erw another place unknown.

thee

thee like a lion foremoft in piercing thy enemies, like a ftrong eagle,
a fafeguard to thy people. Upon this account they will no longer
difpute with thee. They vanifh before thee like the ghofts of ʷ Celyddon. Thou haft taken Gwyddgrug and Dyfnant by force, and
Rhuddlan with it's red borders, and thoufands of thy men overthrew
ˣ Dinbych, ʸ Foelas, and ᶻ Gronant; and the men of Carnarvon
thy friends were bufy in action, and Dinas ᵃ Emreis ftrove bravely in
thy caufe, and they vanquifhed with the renowned ᵇ Morgant at their
head all that ftood before them. Thy pledges know not where to
turn their faces, they cannot enjoy mirth or reft. Thou wert honour-
ably covered with blood, and thy wound is a glory to thee. When
thou didft refift manfully the attack of the enemy, thou wert honoured by thy fword, with thy buckler on thy fhoulders. Thou didft
bravely lead thy forces, the aftonifhment of Lloeger, to the borders
of ᶜ Mechain and Mochnant. Happy was the mother who bore
thee, who art wife and noble, and freely diftributeft rich fuits of
garments, thy gold and filver. And thy Bards celebrate thee for
prefenting them thy bred fteeds, when they fit at thy tables. And
I myfelf am rewarded for my gift of poetry, with gold and diftinguifhed refpect. And fhould I defire of my prince the moon as a
prefent, he would certainly beftow it on me. Thy praife reacheth
as far as ᵈ Lliwelydd, and Llywarch is the man who celebrates with

---

ʷ Celyddon, the Britifh name of that
part of North Britain, called Caledonia
by the Romans.

ˣ Dinbych, Denbigh.

ʸ Foelas, or Y Foel las, i. e. the green
fummit, which is the name of a place in
Denbighfhire, where there is an old fort,
now in the poffeffion of Watkyn Wynn,
Efq. colonel of the Denbighfhire militia,
whofe feat is near it.

ᶻ Gronant, the name of a fort or caftle
in Flintfhire.

ᵃ Dinas Emreis or Emrys, the name of
a place in Snowdon, near Bedd Celhert,
where Gwerthenea attempted to build a
caftle.

ᵇ Morgant, the name of one of Llywelyn's generals.

ᶜ Mochain, a part of Powys.

ᵈ Caer Liwelydd, Carlifle.

his

his songs   -   -   -   -   -   -   -

My praises are not extravagant to thee the prodigy of our age, thou art a prince firm in battle like an elephant. When thou arrivest at the period of thy glory, when thy praises cease to be celebrated by the Bard and the harp, my brave prince, ere thou comest, before thy last hour approaches, to confess thy sins, after thou hast through thy prowess vanquished thy enemies; mayst thou at last become a glorious saint.

VIII. A N

VIII.

A N O D E,

In Five PARTS,

To Llewelyn, the son of Gruffudd, last prince of Wales of the British line, composed by Llygad Gwr, about the year 1270.

I.

I ADDRESS myself to God, the source of joy, the fountain of all good gifts, of transcendent majesty. Let the song proceed to pay it's due tribute of praise, to extol my hero, the prince of [a] Arllechwedd, who is stained with blood, a prince descended from renowned kings. Like Julius Cæsar is the rapid progress of the arms of Gruffudd's heir. His valour and bravery are matchless, his crimson lance is stained with gore. It is natural to him to invade the lands of his enemies. He is generous, the pillar of princes. I never return empty-handed from the North. My successful and glorious prince, I would not ex-change on any conditions. I have a renowned prince, who lays

[a] Arllechwydd a part of Carnarvonshire.

England

England waſte, deſcended from noble anceſtors.   Llywelyn the de-
ſtroyer of thy foes, the mild and proſperous governour of Gwynedd,
Britain's honour in the field, with thy ſceptered hand extended on
the throne, and thy gilt ſword by thy ſide.   The lion of [b] Cemais
fierce in the onſet, when the army ruſheth to be covered with red.
Our defence who ſlighteth alliance with ſtrangers, who with violence
maketh his way through the midſt of his enemies country.   His
juſt cauſe will be proſperous at laſt.   About [c] Tyganwy he has
extended his dominion, and his enemies fly from him with maimed
limbs, and the blood flows over the ſoles of men's feet.   Thou dragon
of [d] Arfon of reſiſtleſs fury, with thy beautiful well-made ſteeds, no
Engliſhman ſhall get one foot of thy country.   There is no Cymro
thy equal.

II.

THERE is none equal to my prince with his numerous troops in
the conflict of war.   He is a generous Cymro deſcended from [e] Beli
Hir, if you enquire about his lineage.   He generouſly diſtributeth
gold and riches.   An heroic wolf from [f] Eryri.   An eagle among
his nobles of matchleſs prowefs; it is our duty to extol him.   He is

---

[b] Cemais, the name of ſeveral places in
Wales.   The Bard means here a cantred of
that name in Angleſea.

[c] Tyganwy, the name of an old caſtle
near the mouth of the river Conway to
the eaſt; it was formerly one of the royal
palaces of Maelgwn Gwynedd, king of
Britain, and was, as our annals relate,
burnt by lightning, ann. 811. but was
afterwards rebuilt, and won by the earls
of Cheſter, who held it for a conſiderable time, but was at laſt retaken by the
princes of North Wales.

[d] Arfon, the country now called Car-
narvonſhire.

[e] Beli.   This was probably Beli Mawr,
to whom our Bards generally traced the
pedigree of great men.

[f] Eryri, Snowdon, which ſome ſuppoſe
derived from Mynydd eryrod, the hill of
eagles, but more probably from Mynydd
yr erry, the hill of ſnow.   Snowdon, in
Engliſh, ſignifies literally the hill of ſnow,
from Snow and Down, that being ſtill a
common name for a hill in England, as
Barham Downs, Oxford Downs, Burford
Downs, &c.

cled

clad in a golden veſt in the army, and ſetteth caſtles on fire. He is the
bulwark of the battle with ⁵ Greidiawl's courage. He is a hero that
with fury breaketh whole ranks, and fighteth manfully. His violence
is rapid, his generoſity overflowing. He is the ſtrength of armies
arrayed in gold. He is a brave prince whoſe territories extend as far
as ʰ Teifi, whom no body dares to puniſh. Llywelyn the vanquiſher
of England is a noble lion deſcended from the race of kings. Thou
art the king of the Mighty, the entertainer and encourager of Bards.
Thou makeſt the crows rejoice, and the ⁱ Bryneich to vomit blood,
they feaſted on their carcaſes. He never avoided danger in the ſtorm
of battle, he was undaunted in the midſt of hardſhips. The ᵏ Bards
propheſy that he ſhall have the government and ſovereign power;
every prediction is at laſt to be fulfilled. The ſhields of his men
were ſtained with red in brave actions from ˡ Pulford to the fartheſt
bounds of ᵐ Cydweli. May he find endleſs joys, and be reconciled
to the Son of God, and enjoy Heaven by his ſide.

ᵍ Greidiawl, the name of a hero mentioned by Aneurin Gwawdrydd in his
Gododin.

ʰ Teifi, the name of a large river in
Cardiganſhire.

ⁱ Bryneich, the men of Bernicia, a
province of the Old Saxons in the North
of England. The inhabitants of Deira
and Bernicia are called by our antient hiſtorians, Gwyr Deifr a Bryneich.

ᵏ It was the policy of the Britiſh princes
to make the Bards foretell their ſuccefs in
war, in order to ſpirit up their people to
brave actions. Upon which account the
vulgar ſuppoſed them to be real prophets.

Hence the great veneration they had for
the prophetical Bards, Myrddin Emrys,
Taliefin, and Myrddin Wyllet. This
accounts for what the Engliſh writers ſay
of the Welſh relying ſo much upon the
prophecies of Myrddin. There are many
of theſe pretended prophefies ſtill extant.
The cuſtom of prophefying did not ceaſe
till Henry the Seventh's time, and the reafon is obvious.

ˡ Pwlffordd, is the name of a place in
Shropſhire. There is a bridge of that
name ſtill in that county.

ᵐ Cydweli, the name of a town, and
Comot, in Carmarthenſhire.

III. WE

III.

We have a prudent prince, his lance is crimſon, his ſhield is ſhivered to pieces; a prince furious in action, his palace is open to his friends, but woe is the lot of his enemies. Llywelyn the vanquiſher of his adverſaries is furious in battle like an outrageous dragon; to be guarded againſt him availeth not, when he cometh hand to hand to diſpute the hardy conteſt. May he that made him the happy governour of Gwynedd and it's towns, ſtrengthen him for length of years to defend his country from hoſtile invaſion. It is our joy and happineſs that we have a brave warrior with prancing ſteeds, that we have a noble Cymro, deſcended from Cambrian anceſtors, to rule our country and it's borders. He is the beſt prince that the Almighty made of the four elements. He is the beſt of governours, and the moſt generous. The eagle of Snowdon, and the bulwark of battle. He pitched a battle where there was a furious conteſt to obtain his patrimony on ⁿ Cefn Gelowydd; ſuch a battle never happened ſince the celebrated action of ᶜ Arderydd.

He is the brave lion of Mona, the kind-hearted Venedotian, the valiant ſupporter of his troops in Bryn Derwyn. He did not repent of the day in which he aſſaulted his adverſaries; it was like the aſſault of a

---

ⁿ Cefn Gelorwydd, is the name of ſome mountain, but where it is ſituated I know not.

ᵒ Arderydd, is the name of a place ſomewhere in Scotland, perhaps, Atterith, about ſix miles from Solway Frith. This battle is mentioned in the Triades, and was fought by Gwenddolau ap Ceidiaw and Aeddan Tradawg, petty princes of the North, againſt Rhydderch Hael, king of Cumbria, who got the battle. Myrddin Wyllt, or Merlin, the Caledonian, was ſeverely handled by Rhydderch Hael, for ſiding with Gwenddolau, his patron, which he complains of in his poem, entitled, Afallennau, or Apple-trees.

hero

hero defcended from undaunted anceftors. I faw a hero difputing with hofts of men like a man of honour in avoiding difgrace. He that faw Llywelyn like an ardent dragon in the conflict of Arfon and [p] Eiddionydd, would have obferved that it was a difficult tafk to with-ftand his furious attack by [q] Drws Daufynydd. No man has ever compelled him to fubmit: May the Son of God never put him to confufion.

IV.

LIKE the roaring of a furious lion in the fearch of prey, is thy thirft of praife, like the found of a mighty hurricane over the de-fart main, thou warlike prince of [r] Aberffraw. Thy ravage is furious, thy impetuofity irrefiftible, thy troops are enterprizing in brave actions, they are fierce and furious like a conflagration. Thou art the war-like prince of [s] Dinefwr, the defence of thy people, the divider of fpoils. Thy forces are comely and neat, and of one language. Thy proud Toledo fword is gilt with gold, and it's edge broke in war. Thou prince of [t] Mathrafal, extenfive are the bounds of thy domi-nions, thou ruleft people of four languages. He ftaid undaunted in battle againft a foreign nation, and it's ftrange language. May the

---

[p] Eiddionydd, now Eifionydd, the name of a Commot, or diftrict, in Carnarvonfhire.

[q] Drws Daufynydd, is the name of a pafs between two hills, but where it lies I know not. Drws Daufynydd fignifies, literally, the door of the two hills. There are many paffes in Wales denominated from Drws, as Drws Ardudwy, Drws y Coed, Bwlch Oerddrws, &c.

[r] Aberffraw, the name of a prince's chief palace in Anglefea.

[s] Dinefwr, the name of the prince of South Wales's palace, pleafantly fituated upon a hill above the river Towi, in Carmarthenfhire, now in the poffeffion of George Rice, of Newton, efquire, member of parliament for that county.

[t] Mathrafal, the feat of the prince of Powys, not far from Pool, in Montgo-meryfhire, now in the poffeffion of the earl of Powys.

great King of Heaven defend the juſt cauſe of the warlike prince of the three provinces.

V.

I make my addreſs to God, the ſource of praiſe, in the beſt manner I am able, that I may extol with ſuitable words the chief of men, who rageth like fire from the flaſhes of lightning, who exchangeth thruſts with the burniſhed ſteel. I ſtand in armour by the ſide of my prince with the red ſpear in the conflict of war, he is a brave fighter, and the foremoſt in action. Llywelyn, thy qualities are noble, I will valiantly make my path broad with the edge of my ſword. May the prints of the hoofs of my prince's ſteeds be ſeen as far as Cornwal. Numerous are the perſons that congratulate him upon this ſucceſs, who is a ſure friend. The lion of Gwynedd, and it's extenſive territories, the governour of the men of Powys, and the South, who hath a general aſſembly of his armed troops at Cheſter, who ravageth Lloegr to amaſs ſpoils. In battle his ſucceſs is certain, in killing, burning, and in overthrowing caſtles. In ᵘ Rhos and Penfro, and in conteſts with the Normans, his impetuoſity prevaileth. The offspring of Gruffudd, of worthy qualities, generous in diſtributing rewards for ſongs. His ſhield ſhines, and the ſtrong lances quickly meet the ſtreams of guſhing gore. He extorteth taxes from his enemies, and claimeth another country, as a ſovereign prince. His noble birth is an ornament to him. He beſiegeth fortified towns, and his furious attacks like thoſe of ʷ Fflamddwyn reach far. He is a proſperous chief with princely qualities, his Bards are comely

---

ᵘ Rhos and **Penfro**, the names of two Cantreds, in Pembrokeſhire.

ʷ **Fflamddwyn**, the name of a Saxon prince, againſt whom Urien, king of Cumbria, and his ſon Owain, fought the battle of Argeed Llwyfein.

about

about his tables.   I have feen him generoufly diftributing his wealth, and his mead-horns filled with generous liquors.   Long may he live to defend his borders with his fharp fword, like Arthur with the lance of fteel.   May he who is lawful king of Cymru endued with princely qualities have his fhare of happinefs at the right hand of God.

IX.

A P O E M,

Intituled the Ode of the Months, composed by Gwilym Ddu of Arfon, to Sir Gruffudd Llwyd, of Tregarnedd and Dinorweg.

Why the Bard called this piece the " Ode of the Months" I cannot guess; but by what he intimates in the poem, which is, that when all nature revives, and the whole animal and vegetable creation are in their full bloom and vigour, he mourned and pined for the decay'd state of his country. The hero he celebrates made a brave but successless attempt to rescue it from slavery. It will not be amiss to give a short account of that inhuman massacre of the Bards made by that cruel tyrant Edward the First, which gave occasion to a very fine Ode by Mr. Grey. Sir John Wynne, of Gwydir, a descendant in a direct line from Owain Gwynedd, mentions this particular, and says, he searched all the records in the Exchequer at Carnarvon, and in the Tower of London, for the antiquities of his country in general, and of his own family in particular. I shall set down his own words, as I find them in a very fair copy of that history lent me by Sir Roger Mostyn, of Gloddaith

and

and Moſtyn, Bart. a perſon no leſs eminent for his generous commu-
nicative temper, than for many other public and private virtues.

" *This is the moſt antient ſong* (i. e. one of *Rhys Goch of Eryri's,*
" *a Bard who flouriſhed A. D.* 1400) *I can find extant of my*
" *anceſtors ſince the reign of Edward the Firſt, who cauſed our Bards*
" *all to be hanged by martial law, as ſtirrers of the people to ſedition*;
" *whoſe example being followed by the governors of Wales until Henry*
" *the Fourth's time, was the utter deſtruction of that ſort of men*; *and*
" *ſithence that kind of people were at ſome further liberty to ſing, and*
" *to keep pedigrees, as in antient time they were wont*; *ſince which time*
" *we have ſome light of antiquity by their ſongs and writings,*" *&c.*

It is not improbable that our Bard might have been one of thoſe
who ſuffered in the cauſe of his country, though he had the good luck
to eſcape Edward's fury. I wiſh I may be ſo happy as to convey ſome
faint idea of his merit to the Engliſh reader. The original has ſuch
touches, as none but a perſon in the Bard's condition could have expreſſed
ſo naturally. However not to anticipate the judicious reader's opinion,
to which I ſubmit mine with all deference, I ſhall now produce ſome
account of this great man, taken from that ſkilful and candid antiquary
Mr. Robert Vaughan of Hengwrt's notes on Dr. Powel's hiſtory of
Wales, printed at Oxford, 1663.

" *Sir Gruffudd Lhwyd, knight, the ſon of Rhys ap Gruffudd ap*
" *Ednyfed Fychan, was a valiant gentleman, but unfortunate,* " *mag-*
" *næ quidem, ſed calamitoſæ virtutis,*" *as Lucius Florus ſaith of*
" *Sertorius. He was knighted by king Edward, when he brought*
" *him the firſt news of his queen's ſafe delivery of a ſon at Car-*
" *narvon Caſtle; the king was then at Rhuddlan, at his parliament*
" *held there. This Sir Gruffudd afterwards taking notice of the*
" *extreme*

" *extreme oppression and tyranny exercised by the English officers, es-*
" *pecially Sir Roger Mortimer, lord of Chirk, and justice of North*
" *Wales, towards his contrymen the Welsh, became so far discontented,*
" *that he broke into open rebellion, verifying that saying of Solomon,*
" *Oppression maketh a wise man mad.*" " *He treated Sir Edward*
" *Bruce, brother to Robert, then king of Scotland, who had con-*
" *quered Ireland, to bring or send over men to assist him in his*
" *design against the English; but Bruce's terms being conceived too*
" *unreasonable, the treaty came to nought; however being desperate,*
" *he gathered all the forces he could, and, in an instant, like a candle*
" *that gives a sudden blaze before it is out, overran all North Wales*
" *and the Marches, taking all the castles and holds; but to little pur-*
" *pose, for soon after he was met with, his party discomfited, and him-*
" *self taken prisoner. This was in the year of our Lord* 1322."

    I thought so much by way of introduction necessary to commemorate
so gallant a person; what became of him afterwards is not mentioned
by our historians. However the following poem remains not only as a
monument of the heroe's bravery, but of the Bard's genius.

BEFORE the beginning of May I lived in pomp and grandeur,
but now, alas! I am deprived of daily support, the time is as
distastrous, as when our Saviour Christ was taken and betrayed.
How naked and forlorn is our condition! We are exposed to anxious
toils and cares. O how heavy is the Almighty's punishment, that
the crimson sword cannot be drawn! I remember how great it's size
was, and how wide it's havock; numerous are now the oppressed
captives who languish in gnashing indignation. Our native Bards
are excluded from their accustomed entertainments. How great a

flop is put to generofity fince a munificent hero, like Nudd [a], is confined in prifon. The valorous hawk of [b] Gruffudd, fo renowned for ravaging and deftroying his enemies, is deplored by the expert Bards, who have loft their feftivity and mirth in the place where mead was drunk. I cannot bear to think of his injurious treatment. His hofpitality has fed thoufands. He is, alafs! in a forlorn prifon, fuch is the unjuft oppreffion of the [c] land of the Angles. Years of forrow have overwhelmed me. I reck not what becomes of the affairs of this world. The Bards of two hundred regions lament that they have now no Protector. This is certain, but a fad truth. Though the unthinking vulgar do not reflect as I do on the time when my eagle fhone in his majefty. I am pierced by the lance of defpair. Hard is the fate of my protector, [d] Gwynedd is in a heavy melancholy mood, it's inhabitants are oppreffed becaufe of their tranfgreffions. Long has the bright fword, that fhone like a torch, been laid afide, and the brave courage of the dauntlefs Achilles been ftopped. The whole pleafant feafon of May is fpent in difmal forrow; and June is comfortlefs and chearlefs. It increafeth my tribulation, that Gruffudd with the red lance is not at liberty. I am covered with chilly damps. My whole fabric fhakes for the lofs of my chief. I find no intermiffion to my pain. May I fink, O Chrift! my Saviour, into the grave, where I can have repofe; for now, alafs! the office of the Bard is but a vain and empty name. I am furprized that my defpair has not burft my heart, and that it is not rent through the

[a] Nudd Hael, or the Generous, one of the three liberal heroes of Britain mentioned in the Triades, and celebrated by Taliefin.

[b] Gruffudd Llwyd, the hero of the poem, was the fon of Rhys, the fon of Gruffudd, the fon of the famous Ednyfed

Fychan, fenefchall to Llywelyn the great, and a brave warrior.

[c] The land of the Angles, i. e. England.

[d] Gwynedd, the name of the country, called by the Romans Venedotia, but by the Englifh North Wales.

midft

ımidſt in twain.　The heavy ſtroke of care aſſails my memory, when
I think of his confinement, who was endowed with the valour of
ᵉ Urien in battle.　My meditation on paſt misfortunes is like that of
the ſkilful ᶠ Cywyrd the Bard of Dunawd ᵍ.　My praiſe to the worthy hero is without vicious flattery, and my ſong no leſs affecting
than his.　My panegyric is like the fruitful genius of ʰ Afan

ᵉ Urien Reged, a famous king of Cumbria, who fought valiantly with the
Saxons, whoſe brave actions are celebrated by Talieſin and Llywarch Hen.
He is mentioned by Nennius, the ancient Britiſh hiſtorian, who wrote about
A. D. 858.　This writer is terribly
mangled by his editors, both at home and
abroad, from their not being verſed in
the Britiſh language.　I have collected
ſome manuſcripts of his hiſtory, but cannot meet a genuine one without the inter-
polations of Samuel Beulom, otherwiſe I
would publiſh it.　I have in my poſſeſſion
many notes upon this author, collected
from ancient Britiſh manuſcripts, as well
as Engliſh writers, who have treated of
our affairs.　This I have been enabled to
do, chiefly by having acceſs to the curious library at Llannerch, by the kind
permiſſion of the late Robert Davies,
eſquire, and ſince by his worthy ſon
John Davies, eſquire, which I take this
opportunity gratefully to acknowledge.

ᶠ Cywryd, this Bard is not mentioned
either by Dr. Davies or Mr. Edward
Llwyd, in their catalogues of Britiſh
writers.　It ſeems he flouriſhed in the
ſixth century, as did all the ancient Britiſh Bards we have now extant.　Here
let me obviate what may be objected to me
as mentioning ſo many facts, and perſons
who lived in the ſixth century, within the
courſe of this performance.　It was the
laſt period our kings fought with any

ſucceſs againſt the Saxons, and it was
natural, therefore, for the Bards of thoſe
times, to record ſuch gallant acts of
their princes, and for their ſucceſſors to
tranſmit them to poſterity.　Every perſon, though but ſlightly verſed in the Britiſh hiſtory of that time, knows that Cadwaladr was the laſt king of Britain.
Since his time there are no works of the
Bards extant till after the conqueſt, as I
have ſhewed in my Diſſertatio de Bardis.

ᵍ Dunawd, the ſon of Pabo Poſt Prydain, one of the heroes of the ſixth century, who fought valiantly with the
Saxons.

ʰ Afan Ferddig, was the Bard of the
famous Cadwallawn, ſon of Cadfan king
of Britain.　I have got a fragment of a
poem of his compoſition on the death of
his patron Cadwallawn; and as far as I
underſtand it, it is a noble piece, but very
obſcure on account of it's great antiquity;
as are the works of all the Bards who wrote
about his time.　It is as difficult a taſk,
for a modern Welſhman to endeavour to
underſtand thoſe venerable remains, as
for a young ſcholar juſt entered upon the
ſtudy of the Greek language to attack
Lycophron or Pindar, without the help
of a dictionary or ſcholiaſt.　How Mr.
Mackpherſon has been able to tranſlate the
Erſe uſed in the time of Oſſian, who lived
a whole century at leaſt before the ear-
lieſt Britiſh Bard now extant, I cannot
comprehend.　I wiſh ſome of thoſe that

Ferddig in celebrating [i] Cadwallwn of royal enterprizes. I can no more sing of the lance, in well-laboured verse. Since thou doest not live, what avails it that the world has any longer continuance? Every region proclaims thy generosity. The world droops since thou art lost. There are no entertainments or mirth, Bards are no longer honoured: The palaces are no longer open, strangers are neglected, there are no caparizoned steeds, no trusty endearing friendship. No, our country mourns, and wears the aspect of Lent. There is no virtue, goodness, or any thing commendable left among us, but vice, dissolute-ness, and cowardice bear the sway. The great and towering strength of [k] Allon is become an empty shadow; and the inhabitants of Arson [l] are become insignificant below the ford of Rheon [m]. The lofty land of Gwynedd is become weak. The heavy blow of care strikes her down. We must now renounce all consolation. We are con-fined in a close prison by a merciless unrelenting enemy; and what avails a bloody and brave contest for liberty.

are well versed in the Erse or Irish lan-guage, would be so kind to the public, as to clear these matters; for I can hard-ly believe that the Erse language hath been better preserved than the British.

[i] Cadwallon, the son of Cadfan, the most victorious king of Britain, fought many battles with the Saxons; and, among the rest, that celebrated one of Meigin, in which he slew Edward king of Mercia, where the men of Powys be-haved themselves with distinguished brave-ry; and had from thence several privi-leges granted them by that brave prince. These privileges are mentioned by Cyn-ddelw Brydydd Mawr, a Powysian Bard, in a poem, intituled Breiniau Gwr Powys,

or the Privileges of the men of Powys, which is in my custody.

[k] Mon, the Mona of the Latins, call-ed by the English Anglesey, in which at a place called Aberffraw, was the palace of the princes of North Wales. The Bard seems here to hint at the loss of Llywelyn ap Gruffudd the last prince of Wales of the British line.

[l] Arvon, the country now called Car-narvonshire.

[m] Rheon, the name of a river in Car-narvonshire, often mentioned by the Bards; but it must have altered it's name since, for I do not recollect any such ri-ver which bears that name at present.

FINIS.

H A V I N G finished the present small collection of the British Bards, I take this opportunity to acquaint the reader, that the time in which they flourished is not accurately set down, by Dr. Davies, at the end of his Dictionary, nor by Mr. Lhwyd, of the Museum, in his Catalogue of British Writers, in the Archæologia Britannica. Indeed it is impossible to be so exact, as to fix the year when the Bards wrote their several pieces, unless the actions they celebrate are mentioned in our Annals, because some of them lived under several princes. This I thought proper to mention, lest any should blame the translator for his inaccuracy, in settling the Chronology of the Poems.

H 2

A short

A short Account of TALIESIN, the Chief of Bards, and ELPHIN, the Son of GWYDDNO GARANIR his Patron.

G Wyddno Garanir, was a petty king of Crantre'r Gwaelod, whose country was drowned by the sea, in a great inundation that happened about the year 560, through the carelessness of the person into whose care the dams were committed, as appears from a poem of Taliesin upon that sad catastrophe. In his time the famous Taliesin lived, whose birth and education is thus related in our ancient manuscripts. He was found exposed in a wear belonging to Gwyddno, the profit of which he had granted to his son, prince Elphin, who being an extravagant youth, and not finding the usual success, grew melancholy; and his fishermen attributed his misfortune to his riotous irregular life. When the prodigal Elphin was thus bewailing his misfortune; the fishermen espied a coracle with a child in it, enwrapped in a leathern bag, whom they brought to the young prince, who ordered care to be taken of him, and when he grew up gave him the best education, upon which he became the most celebrated Bard of his time. The accomplished Taliesin was introduced by Elphin to his father Gwyddno's court, where he delivered him a poem, giving an account of himself, intituled, Hanes Taliesin, or Taliesin's History; and at the same time another to his patron and benefactor Elphin, to console him upon his past misfortune, and to exhort him to put his trust in Divine Providence. This

is

is a fine moral piece, and very artfully addreffed by the Bard, who introduces himfelf in the perfon and character of an expofed infant. As it is probable that the prince's affairs took another turn fince that period; this was done with great propriety. Sir John Price mentions the poem, that Taliefin delivered to king Gwyddno, in his Hiftoriæ Britannicæ defenfio. " Taliefinus quidem in odula, quam " de fuis erroribus compofuit, fic infcripta Britannicè (Hanes Taliefin) " videlicet errores Taliefini, ait fe tandem divertiffe ad reliquias " Trojæ;

" Mi a ddaethum yma at Weddillion Troia."

" neque dubitandum eft hoc fuiffe opus Taliefini : nam præter innu- " meros codices vetuftiffimos, qui infcriptionem hujufmodi atteften- " tur, nullo reclamante, nullus eft recentiorum qui vel phrafin illius " tam antiquam, carminifve majeftatem affequi potuit. Et ideo fum- " mus ille vates inter Britannos cenfetur et nominatur." I never could procure a perfect nor correct copy of this poem of Taliefin, otherwife I would gratify the curious with a tranflation of it. It is certain from his hiftory, that he was a very learned man for his time, and feems to have been well verfed in the doctrine of the Druids, particularly the μετεμψύχωσις, which accounts for the extravagant flights frequent in his poems. I have now in my poffeffion above fifty of them; but they are fo very difficult to be underftood, on account of their great antiquity, and numerous obfolete words, and negligence of tranfcribers, that it is too great a tafk for any man at this diftance of time to go about a tranflation of them. However I have felected this ode, as a fpecimen of his manner of writing, not as it is the beft in the collection, but as it is the only one I could throughly underftand. There are many fpurious pieces fathered upon this Bard, in a great many hands in North Wales; but thefe are all forged either

by

by the monks, to anfwer the purpofes of the church of Rome, or by
the Britifh Bards, in the time of the latter princes of Wales, to fpirit up their countrymen againft the Englifh, which any body verfed
in the language may eafily find by the ftyle and matter. It has been
my luck to meet with a manufcript of all his genuine pieces now
extant, which was tranfcribed by the learned Dr. Davies, of Mallwyd,
from an old manufcript on vellom of the great antiquary Mr. R.
Vaughan, of Hengwrt. This tranfcript I have fhewn to the beft antiquaries and critics in the Welfh language now living. They all
confefs that they do not underftand above one half of any of his
poems. The famous Dr. Davies could not, as is plain from the
many obfolete words he has left without any interpretation in his
dictionary. This fhould be a caveat to the Englifh reader concerning the great antiquity of the poems that go under the name of
Offian, the fon of Fingal, lately publifhed by Mr. Mackpherfon.
It is great pity Taliefin is fo obfcure, for there are many particulars in
his poems that would throw great light upon the hiftory, notions, and
manners of the ancient Britons, efpecially of the Druids, a great part
of whofe learning it is certain he had imbibed. This celebrated Bard
was in great favour with all the great men of his time, particularly
with Maelgwn Gwynedd, the warlike and victorious king of all Britain, with Elphin his patron, whom he redeemed with his fongs
from the caftle of Tyganwy, where he was upon fome account con-
fined by his uncle Maelgwn. He likewife celebrated the victories of
Urien Regen, king of Cumbria, and a great part of Scotland, as
far as the river Clyde. In fhort, he was held in fo great efteem by
pofterity, that the Bards mentioned him with the greateft honour
in their works. In his poem, intituled, Aurheg Urien, or Urien's
prefent, he fays, that his habitation was, by Llyn Geirionnydd, in
the parifh of of Llan Rhychwyn, in Carnarvonfhire, and mentions
therein

therein his cotemporary, the famous Aneirin Gwawdrydd, author of the Gododin, an heroic poem, on the battle of Cattraeth, of which some account is given in the Differtatio de Bardis.

> A wn ni cnw Aneirin Gwawdrydd Awenydd
> A minnau Daliefin o lann Llyn Geirionnydd.

i. e. I know the fame of that celebrated genius Aneirin Gwaw-drydd, who am Taliefin, whofe habitation is by the pool Geirion-nydd. ——

HAVING finifhed this fhort account of our author, I fhall now proceed to his poem, intituled, Dyhuddiant Elphin, or Elphin's Confolation, which I offer now to the public.

DR. John David Rhys quotes it at length in his Linguæ Cymraecæ Inftitutiones Accuratæ; which to fave further trouble I fhall beg leave to tranfcribe here in his own words. "Cæterum nunc " et propter eorum authoritatem, et quod huic loco inter alia maxime " quadrant, non pigebit quædam antiquiffima Taliefini Cambro- " Britannica Carmina fubjungere, &c."

I HAVE nothing more to acquaint the reader with, but that I have ufed two copies in my tranflation, one in print by the faid Dr. John David Rhys, the other in manufcript by Dr. Thomas Williams. I have followed the copy I thought moft correct, and have given the different reading of the manufcript in the margin.

X. TALIESIN's

X.

T A L I E S I N' S   P O E M

To Elphin, the Son of Gwyddno Garanir, king of Cantrer'
Gwaelod, to comfort him upon his ill fuccefs at the Wear;[a]
and to exhort him to truft in Divine Providence.

I.

FAIR Elphin, ceafe to weep, let no man be difcontented with
his fortune; to defpair avails nothing. It is not that which
man fees that fupports him. Cynllo's prayer will not be ineffectual.
God will never break his promife. There never was in Gwyddno's
Wear fuch good luck as to-night.

II.

FAIR Elphin, wipe the tears from thy face ! Penfive melancholy
will never profit thee ; though thou thinkeft thou haft no gain ; certainly too much forrow will do thee no good; doubt not of the
great Creator's wonders ; though I am but little, yet am I endowed
with great gifts. From the feas and mountains, and from the bot-
tom of rivers, God fends wealth to the good and happy man.

---

[a] Wear is made with hurdles, generally either in the fea or near the mouth of
great rivers, to catch fifh.

I   III. Elphin

III.

ELPHIN with the lovely qualities, thy behaviour is unmanly, thou oughteſt not to be over penſive.   To truſt in God is better than to forebode evil.   Though I am but ſmall and ſlender on the beach of the foaming main, I ſhall do thee more good in the day of diſtreſs than three hundred ſalmons.

IV.

ELPHIN with the noble qualities, murmur not at thy misfortune: Though I am but weak on my leathern couch, there dwelleth a gift on my tongue.   While I continue to be thy protection, thou needeſt not fear any diſaſter.   If thou deſireſt the aſſiſtance of the ever bleſſed Trinity, nothing can do thee hurt.

D E

B A R D I S

DISSERTATIO;

IN QUA NONNULLA

Quæ ad eorum antiquitatem et munus reſpiciunt,

Et ad præcipuos qui in CAMBRIA floruerunt,

BREVITER DISCUTIUNTUR.

STUDIO ET OPERA

E V A N I   E V A N S,   Cereticenſis.

Si quid mea carmina poſſunt,
Aonio ſtatuam ſublimi vertice Bardos ;
Bardos Pieridum cultores, atque canentis
Phœbi delicias, quibus eſt data cura perennis
Dicere nobilium clariſſima facta virorum,
Aureaque excelſam fœnam ſuper aſtra locare.

JOH. LELANDUS in Aſſertione ARTURII.

INSIGNI VIRO

GVLIELMO VAVGHAN

DE CORS Y GEDOL ARMIGERO,

ET

IN SENATV BRITANNICO

PRO COMITATV *MEIRIONNYDD* DELEGATO,

PROVINCIAE PRAEFECTO, ROTVLORVM CVSTODI,

SOCIETATIS *CYMMRODORION* LONDINI

PRAESIDI SVMMO,

CAETERISQVE EIVSDEM SOCIETATIS MEMBRIS,

HANC DE *BARDIS* DISSERTATIONEM,

SVMMA, QVA PAR EST, OBSERVANTIA

D. D. D.

EVANVS EVANS.

DE

BARDIS

DISSERTATIO;

QUUM per multos annos non fine fumma voluptate Bardos Britannos horis fubficivis evolverem, et quum hac ætate fere in defuetudinem abiere ejufmodi ftudia, et quicquid eft Britannicæ antiquitatis noftrorum pereat incuriâ, non potui quin hanc qualem qualem rudi Minerva differtatiunculam in vulgus emitterem, quo exteris melius innotefcat, quantum in his olim profecêre noftrates.

BARDI apud Celtas originem habuerunt; et Græci, qui eorum meminerunt, mira omnino de illis produnt, quæ eo magis fidem merentur quod non folebant laudes fuas in Barbaros effufè impendere. Cum alibi gentium hodie nulla eorum maneant veftigia nifi apud Cambro-Britannos et Hibernos, Celtarum pofteros; è re fore duxi, fi aliquid de antiquioribus qui apud nos extant, prælibarem, præmiffis de iis in genere ex Scriptoribus Græcis et Latinis elogiis, quò

auguftius

augustius in scenam prodeant, et inde venerandæ antiquitatis auctoritatem sibi vindicent.

---Unde Bardi nomen sunt sortiti, nondum mihi constat; Annii enim Viterbiensis regem Bardum, uti et omnia ejus hujuscemodi commenta, penitus rejicio. Non omnino abludit vox *Bâr* furor, modo sit ille poeticus quo se agitari fingebant Bardi. Si ea fuerit vocis origo, necesse est ut primitùs scriberetur *Barydd*. Utcunque sit, nos a multis retrò Seculis furorem illum poeticum voce Awen designamus, quæ deduci potest a Gwên, *risus* vel *lætitia:* Poetæ enim munus est ut homines cantu exhilaret. Non multum ergo contendimus an ea sit vocis origo, cum vocabulorum antiquorum, cujusmodi sunt hominum, officiorum, urbium, montium et fluviorum sit admodum obscura significatio.

His de Bardorum origine præmissis, ad eorum pergamus munus, prout Scriptores Græci et Latini tradiderunt. Primus sit Diodorus Siculus, qui hæc scribit. Ἐισὶ καὶ παρ' αὐ]οῖς καὶ ποιη]αὶ μελῶν, ἃς ΒΑΡΔΟΥΣ ὀνεμάζεσι, ἕτοι δὲ μετ' ὀργάνων ταῖς λύραις ὁμείων ἄδον]ες, ἃς μᾶν ὑμνᾶσι, ἃς δὲ βλασφημᾶσι[a]. Non multum dissimile est quod de illis prodit Ammianus Marcellinus. " Bardi (inquit ille) fortia " virorum illustrium facta heroicis composita versibus cum dulcibus " lyræ modulis cantitarunt." His Possidonii apud Athenaeum verba addere lubet, qui eorum munus graphicè depingit. Κελ]ὰ περιάγον]αι μεθ' ἑαυ]ῶν, καὶ πολεμῶντες συμβιω]ὰς ἃς καλᾶσι παρασίτες. ἕτοι δὲ ἐγκώμια αὐ]ῶν, καὶ πρὸς ἀθρόες λέγεσιν ἀνθρώπες συνεςῶτας, καὶ πρὸς ἕκαςον τῶν κα]ὰ μέρος ἐκείνων ἀκροωμένων. τὰ δὲ ἀκέσματα αὐ]ῶν ἐισιν οἱ καλέμ]μοι ΒΑΡΔΟΙ. ποιη]αὶ δὲ ἕτοι τυγχάνεσι μετ' ὠδῆς ἐπαίνες λέγον]ες[b].

[a] P. 213. H. Steph. Edit. 1559.   [b] P. 246. D.

Hinc

Hinc manifesto liquet eorum præcipuum munus fuisse Heroum laudes in coelum evehere. Sed quum nulla Celticorum vel Gallicorum extent Bardorum opera, ex quibus quam dignè munus gesserint evincatur, operæ pretium est, alium ex eodem ATHENAEO locum adducere, ex quo patebit hautquaquam iis defuisse sublime dicendi genus, quod Græci ὕψος vocant. Posidonius, Luernii, qui Bittitis pater fuit à Romanis profligati, opes cùm enarrat, tradit eum popularem gratiam aucupantem, per agros curru vehi solitum, aurúmque et argentum in turbas Celtarum innumeras eum prosequentes spargere : quin et septum eundem quadratum stadiorum duodecim aliquando cinxisse, in quo potione sumptuosa et exquisita pleni lacus essent, paratáque cibariorum copia, ut complusculis diebus liceret iis quibus placeret, ingredi, fruíque illo apparatu, cum assiduis ministrorum officiis. Epularum diem aliquando cùm ille constituisset, ac præfiniisset, barbarum quendam Poetam tardius cæteris eo commeantem illi occurrisse, ac canentem laudes ejus, excellentésque virtutes celebrasse, vicem verò suam doluisse, ac deflevisse, quòd serius adventasset : illum cantu delectatum auri sacculum poposcisse, et accurrenti cantori projecisse : quo sublato, poëtam ejus rursum laudes iterantem prædicasse currûs, quo vehebatur, impressa in terram vestigia aurum et beneficia procreare mortalibus. Sed præstat ipsa ATHENAEI verba apponere.

Ἔτι ὁ Ποσειδώνι۞ δ᾽ ἡγουμϑύλος κỳ τὸν Λουερνίου τῦ Βηύιτος πατρὸς πλοῦτον, τῦ ὑπὶ Ρωμαίων καθαιρεθένῖ۞, φησί, δημαγωγοῦνῖα αὐπὸν τὸς ὄχλους ἐν ἅρμαῖ, φέρεῶ διὰ τ πεδίων, κỳ σπείρειν χρυσόν, κỳ ἄργυρον τ ἀκολουθούσαις τ Κελτῶν μυριάσι, φράγμα τε ποιεῖν δωδεκαςάδιον τετράγωνον, ἐν ᾧ πληροῦν λάκκ۞ πολυτελοῦς πόμαῖ۞, παρασκευάζειν τε ποσ᾽ τι ῥωμάτων πλῆθ۞, ὥστ᾽ ἐφ᾽ ἡμέρας πλείονας ἐξεῖναι τοῖς βουλομϑύοις τῶν παρασκευασθέντων ἀπολαύειν, ἀδιαλείπτως διακονουμϑύοις. Ἀφορίσανῖος δ᾽ αὐτὰ προθεσμίαν ποτὲ τῆς θοίνης, ἀφυστερήσανῖά τινα τῶν βαρβάρων ποιητὴν ἀφικέσθαι, καὶ συναντήσανῖα μετ᾽ ᾠδῆς ὑμνεῖν αὐτῦ τὴν ὑπεροχὴν, ἑαυτὸν δ᾽ ἀποδύρεσθαι ὅτι ὑστέρηκε τ ᾿ δὲ ᾀσθέντα

K

θυλάκιον αἴῆσαι χρυσίx, καὶ ῥίψαι αὐῖῷ παραῖρέχϾῆι, ἀνελόμβμον δ᾽ ἐκεῖνον πάλιν ὑμνεῖν, λέγοῆα, ΔΙΟΤΙ ΤΑ ΙΧΝΗ ΤΗΣ ΓΗΣ (ΕΦ ΗΣ ΑΡΜΑ-ΤΗΛΑΤΕΙ) ΧΡΥΣΟΝ ΚΑΙ ΕΥΕΡΓΕΣΙΑΣ ΑΝΘΡΩΠΟΙΣ ΦΕΡΕΙᶜ.

Haec funt quæ (ut pote cui ad Bibliothecas aditus non patet) de antiquis illis in medium proferre licuit. Ad noftros jam venio in quibus non defunt veri et genuini ὕψϾϾ exempla. Nequaquam fuo genere Græcis et Latinis poetis cedunt noftri Bardi, quamvis ad eorum normam carmina non texerunt. Quid enim nobis cum exteris? An eorum modulo et pede noftra poemata metenda funt? Quid, ut taceam de Arabicis et Brachmanicis, et in Europa boreali Scaldis? quid fiet, inquam, de antiquioribus illis Sacrofanctis poetis? quid fiet de Jobo, Davide, et fiqui alii θεοδίδακῖοι poetæ? Sed hæc a propofito noftro aliena funt.

Quum res Britonum, ingruentibus Pictis, Scotis, et Saxonibus, laberentur, dici non poteft, quantam libris et veteribus noftrorum monumentis ftragem ediderint: adeo ut Bardi et hiftorici verè antiqui, fint admodum rari. E noftris hiftoricis qui Bardorum meminit, primus eft Gildas Nennius, qui fcripfit, uti ipfe narrat, anno 858, et quarto Mervini regis. Sed is locus in nonnullis exemplaribus deeft, et ejus auctor clariffimo Vaughano, Nennio antiquior effe videtur, qui eum " vetuftum Saxonicæ genealogiæ autorem" nominat. Sive verò is fuerit Nennius, quod mihi videtur, five, uti ille mavult, aliquis eo vetuftior, omnia quæ ibi narrantur quam veriffima funt, quamvis fcribentium ofcitantia quam fœdiffime fint depravata. Nec mendas caftigarunt editores Gale et Bertram. Quæ ad Bardos fic fe habent. " Item Taliaiarn Tatangen in " poemate claruit, et Nuevin, et Taliesin, et Bluchbar, et " Cian

" Cian qui vocatur Gweinchgwant, fimul uno tempore in
" poemate Britannico claruerunt." Qui locus fic reftitui debet.
" Item Talhaiarn Tatangwn claruit, et Aneurin, et Ta-
" liesin, et Llywarch, et Cian qui vocatur Gwyngwn fimul
" uno tempore in poemate Britannico claruerunt." Ex iis quos hic
nominat Nennius tres tantum extant, nempe Aneurin, Taliesin
et Llywarch cognoménto Hen. Meminit tamen Talhaiarni
Taliesinus in poemate cui titulus *Angar Cyfyndawd*, i. e. *Concordia
difcors*.

Trwy jaith Talhaiarn,
Bedydd bi dlydd Jarn.

" Ex Talhaiarni fententia.
Expiatio erit per baptifmum in die fupremo.",

Uti et Ciani in eodem poemate.

Cian *pan ddarfu*
Lliaws gyfolu.

" Quando Cianus multos carmine celebraret."

Meminit et ejudem Aneurinus in fuo poemate Heroico, cui nomen
Gododin.

Un maban y Gian o faen Gwyngwn.

" Unicus Ciani filius ex valido *Gwyngwn* ortus."

Sed

Sed quum eorum opera aboleverit aetas, nihil ultra de iis dicere poſſumus. Hoc ſaltem conſtat, ſi NENNIO fides adhibenda ſit, eos ſuo ſeculo Bardos fuiſſe eximios. ANEURINUS, TALIESINUS et LLY- WARCH HEN habent multa notatu digna, et quæ rei iſtius ſeculi hiſtoricæ multum lucis adferunt. Sed quum eorum ſint rariſſima exemplaria, intellectu ſunt quam difficillima, quod ſit partim ob ſcribentium oſcitantiam, partim ob linguam vetuſtam et obſoletam, quæ in nullo Lexico vel gloſſario inveniri poteſt. Unde ſit, ut ſæpe ſen plus dimidio vel a peritiſſimo intelligatur. TALIESINUS quem noſtrates *Pen Beirdd*; i. e. Bardorum Coryphæum appellavere, in aulis Britanniæ principum vixit, et ibi clara eorum in bello facinora cantavit. Patronos habuit MAELGWN GWYNEDD, eum ſcilicet quem GILDAS MAGLOCUNUM vocat; et URIENUM Regedenſem Cumbriæ principem et ELPHINUM filium GWYDDNO. GARANIR Dominum *Cantref Gwaelod*, cujus regio a mari abſorpta eſt circa an- num 540. Floruerunt TALIESINUS et ANEURIN GWAWDRYDD *Mychdeyrn Beirdd*, i. e. Bardorum Monarcha, eodem tempore, circa annum 570. ANEURINUS, in ſuo poemate cui titulus *Gododin*, refert ſe in bello juxta *Cattraeth* ſub auſpiciis MYNYDDAWC EIDDIN, bellum adverſus Saxones geſſiſſe, et ibi omnes, tribus exceptis, inter quos erat ANEURINUS, bello occubuiſſe. Fuerunt ſub hoc principe in hac expeditione trecenti et ſexaginta tres viri nobiles, qui eum ad bellum juxta *Cattraeth* ſunt ſecuti. Fit hujus exercitus mentio in libro *Triadum* in hunc modum. Teir goſgordd addwyn Ynys *Prydain*. Goſgordd MYNYDDAWG EIDDIN Yng *Cattraeth*; a goſgordd ME- LYN a CHYNFELYN; a goſgordd DRYWON mab NUDD yn *Rhod- wydd Arderydd*. i. e. Tres fuere nobiles exercitus Inſulæ Britannicæ. Exercitus MYNYDDAWG EIDDIN juxta *Cattraeth*; Exercitus ME-

LYN et **CYNFELYN**; et Exercitus **DRYWON** filii **NUDD** juxta *Rhodwydd Arderydd.*

PLACUIT hic nonnulla ex ANEURINI *Gododinio* excerpere, quæ licet ob vetuſtatem et dialecti varietatem ſint admodum obſcura (fuit enim ſi non Pictorum lingua, ſaltem Britannorum ſeptentrionalium dialectus, et ideo hodiernis Cambro-Britannis minus facilis intellectu) attamen lectori haud injucunda fore judicavi, eo quod ſalvis Græcis et Latinis ſit forſan antiquiſſimum in Europâ poema. Interpretationem in multis claudicare nullus dubito. Iı quibus plura exemplaria videre contigerit, ea felicius enucleabunt. Ego non niſi unum vidi a THOMA GULIELMO Medico practico ſcriptum, in quo quæ ſequuntur ſic ſe habebant.

> CAEAWG CYNHORAWG myn yd elai,
> Diphun ym mlaen bun medd a dalai,
> Twll tal i rodawr yn i clywai awr,
> Ni roddai nawd maint dilynai,
> Ni chilia o gamawn, yn i ſerai
> Waed mal brwyn, gomynei wyr nid elai,
> Nis adrawdd Gododin ar llawr MORDAI,
> Rhag pebyll MAELOG pan atcorei
> Namyn un gwr o gant yn y ddelai.

i. e.

> " CAEAWG CYNHORAWG ubicunque ivit,
> " - - - - - hydromeli dedit,
> " Scutum ejus fuit perforatum, ubicunque audivit
> " Clamorem, hoſtibus non pepercit, et eos inſecutus eſt
> " Ne.

" Nec prius a bello destitit, quam sanguis effuse fluxerit,
" Et eos qui non discedebant securi percussit ;
" Adeo ut non possit Gododin celebrare facta in aula MORDAI.
" Ex MADOCI castris quum domum profectus est
" Unus tantum ex centum rediit."

CADAWG CYNHORAWG arfawg yngawr,
CYNO diwygwr gwrdd yngwyawr,
Cynran yn rhagwan rhag byddinawr,
Cwyddai bum pumwnt rhag eu llafnawr,
O wyr *Deifr* a *Bryneich* dychrawr,
Ugeincant eu difant yn unawr,
Cynt i gig i fleidd nog yt i neithiawr,
Cynt e fydd i fran, nog yt i elawr,
Cyn noe argyfrein e waed i lawr,
Gwerth medd ynghyntedd gan *Llwveddawr*,
HYFEIDD HIR ermygir tra fo Cerddawr.

i. e.

" CAEAWG CYNHORAWG vir in bello armatus,
" Et CYNO qui se strenuum gessit in dimicando,
" Ceciderunt numerus ingens eorum hastis transfixi.
" Prius lupo parabatur caro, quam nuptiali convivio ;
" Et corvo prius commodum fuit, quam Libitinæ.
" Prius quam humi fluebat ejus sanguis
" In aula *Lliweddawr* mulfum bibit,
" Et HYFEIDD HIR celebrabitur, donec erit Cantor."

ᶜ Deipnof. p. 152.

Gwyr

Gwyr a aeth *Gattraeth* feddfaeth feddwn,
Ffurf ffrwythlawn, oedd cam nas cymhwyllwn,
I am lafnawr coch, gorfawr, gwrmwn,
Dwys dengyn ydd ymleddyn aergwn,
Ar deulu *Bryneich* be ich barnafwn,
Diluw, dyn yn fyw nis gadawfwn,
Cyfeillt a gollais, difflais oeddwn,
Rhugl yn ymwrthryn, rhyn rhiadwn.
Ni mynnws gwrawl gwaddawl chwegrwn,
Maban y GIAN o faen GWYNGWN.

i. e.

" Viri feftinabant *Cattraeth*, quibus mulfum erat potus,
" Formâ eximii, quibus ingratus eſſem, ſi non meminerim.
" Haftis armati turmatim rubris, magnis et incurvatis,
" Pugnabant impetuoſi bellatores.
" Si mihi liceret [a] fententiam de *Deirorum* populo ferre,
" Æque ac diluvium omnes una ſtrage proſtrarem;
" Amicum enim amiſi incautus,
" Qui in refiftendo firmus erat   –   ꞊   ꞉
" Non petiit magnanimus dotem a focero,
" Filius CIANI ex ſtrenuo GWYNGWN ortus."

[a] Fortaſſe, " Vindictam in Deirorum populum," &c.

Yfeis

Yfeis i o win a medd y MORDAI,
Mawr maint i wewyr,
Ynghyfarfod gwyr,
Bwyd i eryr eryfmygai.
Pan gryffiei GYDYWAL cyfddwyreai
Awr, gan wyrdd wawr cyn i dodai,
Aeffawr ddellt am bellt a adawai,
Parrau ryn rwygiad, dygymmynai
Ynghat blaen bragat briwai.

i. e.

" Ego bibi ex vino et Mulfo MORDAI,
" Cujus hafta fuit immanis magnitudinis.
" In belli congreffu,
" Victum aquilis paravit.
" Quando CYDYWAL feftinavit, exortus eft clamor
" Ante croceam auroram, cum fignum dedit,
" Scutum in afferes comminutos fregit,
" Et haftis lacerantibus percuffit,
" Et in bello eos qui primam ftationem funt nacti vulneravit.

Gwyr a aeth Gattraeth buant enwawd;
Gwin a medd o aur fu eu gwirawd,
Blwyddyn yn erbyn wrdyn ddefawd,
Trywyr a thriugaint a thrichant eurdorchawd,
O'r fawl yt gryffiaffant uch gormant wirawd,
Ni ddiengis namyn tri o wrhydri ffoffawd,
Dau gatei Aeron, a CHYNON DAEARAWD
A minnau o'm gwaedffreu gwerth fy ngwenwawd.

" Viri

i. e.

" Viri ibant ad CATTRAETH, et fuere infignes,
" Vinum et mulfum ex aureis poculis erat eorum potus.

\- \- \- \- \- \- \- \-

" Trecenti et fexaginta tres aureis torquibus infigniti erant,
" Ex iis autem qui nimio potu madidi ad bellum properabant,
" Non evafere nifi tres, qui fibi gladiis viam muniebant,
" Sc. bellator de *Acron* et CONANVS DAEARAWD,
" Et egomet ipfe (fc. Bardus Aneurinus) fanguine rubens,
" Aliter ad hoc carmen compingendum non fuperftes fuiffem.

Pan gryffiei GARADAWG i gad,
Mab baedd coed, trychwn, trychiad,
Tarw byddin yn nhrin gymmyniad,
Ef llithiai wydd gwn oi angad,
Ys fy nhyft EWEIN fab EULAD,
A GWRIEN, a GWYN, a GWRIAD,
O *Gattraeth* o gymmynad,
O *Fryn Hydwn* cyn caffad,
Gwedi medd gloyw ar angad,
Ni weles WRIEN ei dad.

i. e.

" Quando ad bellum properabat CARADOCUS,
" Filius apri fylveftris qui truncando mutilavit hoftes,
" Taurus aciei in pugnæ conflictu,
" Is lignum (i. e. haftam) ex manu contorfit,
" Cujus rei funt teftes EWEIN filius EULAD,
" Et GWRIEN et GWYN et GWRIAD.

L

" Ex

" Ex *Cattraeth* et congreſſu ibi,
" Ex *Bryn Hydwn* ubi prius habitavit, oriundus,
" Poſtquam mulſum lucidum in manu tenuerat,
" Non vidit patrem ſuum Gwrienus.

Cyfwyrein cetwyr cyfarfuant,
Ynghyt, yn unfryt yt gyrchaſſant,
Byrr eu hoedl, hir eu hoed ar eu carant,
Seith gymmaint o Loegrwys a laddaſſant,
O gyfryſſedd gwragedd gwych a wnaethant,
Llawer mam ai deigr ar ei hamrant.

i. e.

" Laudo bellatores qui congreſſi ſunt omnes,
" Et uno animo hoſtes adorti ſunt,
" Fuit eorum vita brevis, et longum amicis deſiderium reliquerunt,
" Occiderunt tamen ex Saxonibus plus ſcepties
" ᵇ Ex contentione mulierum egregiè egerunt,
" Et frequens erat mater lacrymas profundens.

Arddyledawc canu, cymman o fri,
Twrf tân, a tharan, a rhyferthi,
Gwryd ardderchawg marchawg myſgi,
Rhudd Fedel rhyfel a eidduni,
Gwr gwnedd, difuddiawg, dygymmyni ynghat,
O'r meint gwlad yt glywi.

ᵇ Quid ſibi vult hic Bardus non mihi conſtat.

5

" Debitas

i. e.

" Debitus eſt tibi cantus, qui honorem aſſecutus ſes maximum,
" Qui eras inſtar ignis, tonitrui et tempeſtatis,
" Viribus eximie, eques bellicoſe
" RHUDD FEDEL, bellum meditaris.
" Licet vir ſtrennuus adoriatur, eum ſuperabis in bello
" Ex quacunque regione eum adveniſſe audieris.

Arddyledawc canu claer orchorddion,
A gwedi dyrraith dyleinw afon,
Dimcones loſlen ben eryron llwyd,
Ef gorau bwyd i yſglyfion.
Or a aeth *Gattraeth* o aurdorchogion,
Ar neges MYNYDDAWG mynawg Maon,
Ni ddoeth yn ddiwarth o barth Frython,
Ododin wr bell well no CHYNON.

i. e.

" Carmine debent celebrari nobiles proceres,
" Qui poſt conflictum amnes ripas ſuperare ᶜ fecerunt.
" Ejus manus ſatiavit aquilarum fuſcarum gulas,
" Is et optime cibum paravit avibus rapacibus,
" Ex omnibus enim eis qui ibant ad *Cattraeth* aureis torquibus inſigniti,
" Qui partem MYNYDDAWG in bello defendebant clari ſatellites,
" Nullus ex Britonibus melius ſuum egit munus
" In *Gododin*, (ex iis qui ex longinquo venerunt) quam CONANUS.

ᶜ Sc. cruore fuſo.

L 2   Truan

Truan yw gennyf i gwedi lludded
Goddef gloes angau trwy anghyffred
Ag eil trwm truan gennyf fi, gweled
Dygwyddaw an gwyr ni pen o dräed
Ac uchenaid hir ag eilywed
Yn ol gwyr pybyr tymyr tudwed
RHYFAWN a GWGAWN GWIAWN a GWLYGED
Gwyr gorſaf gwriaf gwrdd ynghaled
Ys deupo eu henaid hwy wedi trined
Cynnwys yngwlad nef addef afreued.

i. e.

" Me maximè dolet poſt laborem amicos noſtros
" Subire mortis angorem more inaſſueto;
" Et iterum me maximè dolet quod ipſe vidi
" Viros noſtros in bello gradatim cadentes.
" Gemitus eſt longus et opprobrium
" Poſt homines alacres patriæ decus,
" RHYFAWN et GWGAWN GWIAWN et GWLYGED,
" Viri qui erant ſuſtentacula (belli ſc.) fortiſſimi et in anguſtiis magnanimi
" Aſcendant eorum animæ poſt pugnam
" In regnum cœlorum ubi habitatio eſt ſine ullo deſiderio.

Hæc de ANEURINO ſufficiant.

FLORUERE eodem ſeculo et multi alii Bardi inter quos eminet
MYRDDIN WYLLT, id eſt, MERLINUS Sylveſtris, qui poema com-
poſuit cui titulus *Afallennau*, id eſt, pomarium, in quo patroni ſui
GWENDDOLAU filii CEIDIO munificentiam prædicat.

Afallen

Afallen beren bren y fydd fad
Nid bychan dy lwyth fydd ffrwyth arnad
A minnau wyf cfnawg amgelawg am danad
Rhag dyfod y coedwyr coed gymmynad
I gladdu dy wra dd a llygru dy hád
Fal na thyfo byth afal arnad
A minnau wyf gwyllt gerthrychiad
Im cathrid cythrudd nim cudd dillad
Neum rhoddes Gwenddoleu tlyfau yn rhad
Ac yntau heddyw fal na buad..

i. e.

" O arbos pomifera, dulcis et bona,
" Non parvum fers onus fruȼtuum ;
" Ego tui caufa anxius et folicitus fum;
" Ne lignatores arbores ad cædendas veniant,
" Et effodiant tuam radicem, et femen corrumpant,
" Ita ut nunquam poftea pomum feras:
" Ego fum ferus, hominibus fpeȼtaculum,
" Me occupat horor, et veftes me non amiciunt,
" Genddolau dedit mihi gratìs jocularia,
" Et ipfe eft hodie non uti olim fuit.

Fuit Merlinus Morfrynii filius et Albania oriundus, et alter fuit a Merlino Ambrosio qui vixit tempore Vortigerni, et eò quod nepotem cafu interfecerit in infaniam incidit et in Caledoniam receffit fylyam feri inftar, ubi, cum animi compos effet, fortem fuam carminibus deploravit.

Floruit

Floruit hoc feculo et Llywarch-hen, i. e. longævus, Urien Cambriæ principis confobrinus. Extant ab eo fcripta poemata in quibus narrat fe a Saxonibus in Povifiam pulfum fuiffe, et fibi fuiffe viginti quatuor filios aureis torquibus infignitos, et omnes patriam de-fendendo bello occubuiffe. Qui plura de hoc viro nobili et Bardo defiderat Cl. Llwydii Archæologiam Britannicam confulat p. 259.

Vixerunt eodem tempore alii Bardi, fed cum eorum non ex-tent opera, nomina tantum interferere fufficiat. Tristfardd, Bardd Urien Reged. Dygynnelw, Bardd Owain ap Urien. Afan Ferddig, Bardd Cadwallon ap Cadfan. Golyddan, Bardd Cadwaladr Fendigaid. Sunt in iis qui extant multa quæ hiftorico Britannico ufui effe poffunt : fuere enim Bardi rerum geftarum fidi narratores. Fuit eorum præcipuum munus principum et magnatum laudes, et egregia in bello acta carminibus celebrare, quod et olim de iis obfervavit Lucanus

> Vos quoque, qui fortes animas belloque peremptas
> Laudibus in longum vates dimittitis ævum,
> Plurima fecuri fudiftis carmina Bardi. Lib.

" Bardi (inquit Lelandus in Affertione Arturii) foli muficis " numeris, et illuftri nobilium memoriæ confervandæ ftudebant, cane-" bant illi ad lyram heroum inclyta facta, profuit hoc ftudium mirificè " cognitioni, tanquam per manus pofteritati traditæ. Unde quoque " contigit ut Arturii maximi nomen, fama, gloria utcunque con-" ferventur." Inventus eft enim ejus fepulchrum in monafterio Glafto-nienfi juxta id quod Bardus cecinerat eoram Henrico Secundo, quod

fatis

fatis demonſtrat illos hiſtoricorum fidorum æquè ac poetarum munus egiſſe.

HABEMUS præter hos quos ſupra citavimus Bardos, nonnulla carmina anonyma pervetuſta, quæ Druidum eſſe exiſtimavit EDVARDUS LLUYD, cujuſmodi ſunt *Englynion yr Eiry, y bidiau, y gorwynnion.* Moris fuiſſe Druidis carmina alumnos docere notavit CAESAR : " Magnum ubi verſuum numerum edicere dicuntur. Itaque non-" nulli annos vicenos in diſciplina permanent, neque fas eſſe exiſti-" mant ea litteris mandare, quum in reliquis fere rebus publicis pri-" vatiſque rationibus, Græcis litteris utuntur. Id mihi duabus de " cauſis inſtituiſſe videntur ; quod neque in vulgus diſciplinam efferri " velint, neque eos qui diſcunt litteris confiſos minus memoriæ ſtu-" dere, quod fere pleriſque accidit ut præſidio litterarum diligentiam " in diſcendo ac memoriam remittant." Genus carminis quo in his uſi ſunt fuit *Englyn Milwr.*

HAEC de antiquiſſimis quæ nunc extant Bardis Britannicis dicere ſufficiat, ad illos nunc accedo qui durante Principum Cambriæ gubernaculo floruerunt. A ſeculo ſexto ad decimum nihil quod novi extat ſcriptum, ſaltem non vidi, neque quid cauſæ eſſe potuit augurari poſſum, niſi frequens bellorum ſtrages et Britannorum inter diſſidia. In HOELI BONI, noſtris HYWEL DDA, legibus fit Bardi aulici mentio, et quænam fuerit ejus ibi conditio, [d] quæ, temporis ratione habitâ, fuit perhoneſta. Circa annum 1170 GRUFFUDD AP CONAN Cam-

---

[d] " Qui Harpatorem in manum per-" cuſſerit, componat illum quartâ parte " majori compoſitione quàm alteri ejuſ-" dem conditionis homini." Inter Legg. Ripuariorum et Weſinorum a Lindenbro-chio collectas—Unde patet quanto in honore apud exteros etiam Bardus et Harpator (idem enim plerunque fuit munus) habitus eſſet. Præter harpam aliud inſtrumenti genus ſibi peculiare Norwallen-briæ.

briæ princeps legem Bardis præfcripfit, in qua cautum erat ut nullam præter fuam exercerent artem, in qua et dona et pœnas conftituit. Eos autem in tres claffes divifit, *Prydydd*, *Teuluwr* et *Clerwr*; et fixum unicuique fecundum ordinem ftatuit ftipendium. Eorum electio fieri folebat in folenni principum et procerum conceffu, ubi unicuique fecundum meritum affignatus eft locus. Ille vero qui præcelliat, fellâ donatus eft aureâ vel argenteâ, unde et *Cadeirfardd* dictus, i. e. Bardus qui fellam affecutus eft.

AB eo tempore multi eximii floruerunt Bardi, et a principibus admodum fovebantur. MEILIR qui fuit GRUFFINI filii CONANI Bardus, fuit et ejufdem miles et legatus uti et ipfe in ejus epicedio refert.

> Yfeis gan deyrn o gyrn eurawg
> Arfod faedd feiddiad angad weiniawg
> Yn llys *Aberffraw* er ffaw ffodiawg
> Bum o du Gwledig yn lleithawg
> Eilwaith ydd eithum yn negeffawg
> O leufer lliw camawn iawn dywyffawg
> Bu fedd aur gylchwy yn fodrwyawg
> Torrefid gormes yn llyngheffawg
> Gwedi tonnau gwyrdd gorewynnawg
> Dyphuthynt eu feirch meirch rhygyngawg.

fes vindicant, quod *Crwdd* vocant—Hinc verbum Anglicum *Crowdero* apud Hudibraftum pro *Fiddler or Player upon the Fidlin*, ad quod *Crwdd* principium dediffe videtur. Hoc inftrumenti genus ferè in defuetudinem abiit, et *violino* ceffit.—Ex fex chordis felinis conftat, nec eodem modo quo *violinum* modulatur, quamvis a figurâ haud multùm abludat: In Sudwalliâ penitus ignoratur:

" Romanufque Lyrâ plaudat tibi, Barbarus Harpâ,
" Græcus Achilliaca, *Crotta Britanna* canat."

VENANTIUS. Lib. 7. Carm. 8.

" Dedit

i. e.

" Dedit mihi potum ex cornu deaurato princeps,
" Cujus impetus erat inſtar apri ferocis in bello, cujus
" Manus erat liberalis
" In aula *Aberffraw,* quod mihi decus et felicitas fuit.
" Ex domini mei parte miles fui,
" Et iterum legationem obii.
" Quum a bello cruento diſcederet princeps egregius.
" Mulſo ex poculo aureo bibebatur in circulo,
" Hoſtium enim invaſionem navalem repulimus,
" Et poſt refluxionem undarum viridium perſpumoſarum
" Portabant phaleras in littore ſicco equi geſtientes.

Nec dedignati ſunt ipſi principes hanc artem, animi relaxandi cauſa, colere, ut teſtantur Oweni Cyfeiliog principis *Poviſiæ* et Hoeli filii Oweni *Venedotiæ* principis opera, quibus addere licet Llewellinum ultimum Cambriæ principem. De eo enim ſic Matt. West. circa natale domini Llewellinus acceſſit ad regem miſericordiam non juſtitiam petiturus—et paulo poſt—Rex Edwardus vocalem principem diligenter inſtructum ad partes Walliæ redire permiſit[a]. Poematum argumenta erant egregia in bello facinora, libertas, hoſpitalitas et munificentia, et ſi quæ alia virtus, quæ homines domi ornat, et foris hoſtibus tremendos reddit. Et fuit eorum in accendendis hominum ad clara incepta animis tanta vis, ut nihil æque ſonaret Tyrtæi muſa quum ſuos ad honeſtam mortem oppetendam hortaretur. Et quænam, quæſo, reipublicæ tam utilis virtus, quum hoſtibus utrinque premeretur, et cum ſola ſpes, ſalus et libertas eſſet in armis, quam magnanimus periculorum contemptus, et ad

[a] Vid. Prynne's Coll. of Records, Vol. III. p. 1214.

ea adeunda ardor egregius ? Sed præftat GIRALDUM CAMBRENSEM
audire qui iis vixit temporibus, et fuit eorum quæ hic narrantur ocu-
latus teftis.   " Nec ullo prorfus nifi martio labore vexantur, patriæ
" tamen tutelæ ftudent et libertatis : Pro patria pugnant, pro liber-
" tate laborant ; pro quibus non folum ferro dimicare, verum etiam
" vitam dare dulce videtur.   Unde et in thoro turpe, in bello mori
" decus putant. Ac illud poetæ dixerunt—*procul hinc avertite pacem,*
" *nobilitas cum pace perit,* nec mirum fi non degenerant.   Quorum
" enim hi reliquiæ funt olim, Æneadæ in ferrum pro libertate ruebant.
" De his igitur fpectabile, quod nudi multoties cum ferro veftitis,
" inermes cum armatis, pedites cum equitibus congredi non verentur,
" in quo plerumque conflictu fola fiunt agilitate, et animofitate
" victrices. Illis quorum poeta fic meminit, ficut fitu fic natura
" non diffimiles."

    —————— Populus quos defpicit arctos
    Felices errore fuo, quos ille timorum
    Maximus haud urget leti metus, inde ruendi
    In ferrum mens prona viris, animæque capaces
    Mortis, et ignavum redituræ parcere vitæ.

ET nonnullis interjectis —— " Illud in hoc loco notandum vide-
" tur, quod Anglorum Rex *Henricus* Secundus noftris diebus impe-
" ratori Conftantinoplitano *Emmanueli* fuper infulæ Britannicæ fitu ac
" natura, magifque notabilibus litteris et nunciis inquirenti : Inter
" cætera hoc quafi præcipue notabile refcripfit. In quadam infulæ
" parte funt gentes quæ Wallenfes dicuntur, tantæ audaciæ et fero-
" citatis ut nudi cum armatis congredi non vereantur, adeo ut fan-
" guinem pro patria fundere promptiffime, vitamque velint pro laude
" pacifci." Hactenus GIRALDUS.

    5

Non immerito Bardis tantus fuit habitus honor; ii enim heroum inclyta canentes acta, et majorum illuftria proponentes exempla fuos ad ardua incitabant, unde et patriæ falutem, principibus et proceribus gloriam conciliabant; nec folum illuftria aliorum canebant facta, verum ipfi in bello eodem quo in cantibus ardore incitati, multa præclara fortitudinis exhibebant documenta. GWALCHMAI filius MEI-LIR fe Cambriæ fines adverfus Anglos defendiffe gloriatur in poemate cui titulus *Gorhoffedd* GWALCHMAI, i. e. *ejus Deliciæ*. Stationem ejus juxta fluvium *Efurnwy* fuiffe docet non procul ab agro *Salopienfi*. Sunt multa in hoc poemate tam heroe quam Bardo digna. Poftquam enim excubias per noctem totam egiffet GWALCHMAI, ad lucem diei appropinquantis lætus, loci et rerum circumjacentium pulchritudine delectatus, omnem curam et folicitudinem amovit, et philomelæ cantui, et aquæ juxta labantis murmuri, et arborum herbarumque virori attendit, imminens ab hofte periculum contemnens, Marti æque ac Mercurio paratus, firmum mehercle et generofum pectus!

Poema in hunc modum incipit.

Mochddwyreawg Huan haf dyffeftin
Maws llafar adar, mygr, hyar hin.
Mi ydwyf eurcdeddf ddiofn yn nhrin
Mi wyf llew rhag llu, lluch fy ngorddin
Gorwyliais nos yn achadw ffin
Gorloes rydau dwfr ᶜ *Dygen Freiddin*
Gorlas gwellt didryf, dwfr neud jeffin
Gwylain yn gware ar wely lliant
Llcithrion eu puawr, pleidiau eddrin.

ᶜ *Dygen Freiddin*, hodie *Craeg Freiddin*, eft rupes alta et prærupta in agr. *Salopienfi*, non procul a *Sabrina*.

" O fol

i. e.

" O fol æftive, cito oriens propera,

" Suavis eft cantus avium, et cælum fudum et ferenum eft.

" Ego fum bona indole præditus, et in bello intrepidus,

" Sum leo ftrenuus in fronte exercitus, et meus impetus eft violentus,

" Totam noctem pervigilavi fines tutando

" Ubi funt vada tranflucida juxta *Dygen Freiddin*

" Ubi herba in loco folitario crefcens perviridis eft, et aqua limpida

" Mergi ludunt in fluctuum lecto,

" Quorum plumæ fulgent, et ipfi inter fe certant.

Non pigebit hic de alio Bardo, fcilicet CYNDDELW Brydydd Mawr, i. e. Condelao vate eximio, nonnulla ex Oweni *Venedotiæ* principis epicedio excerpere; fuit enim ille, uti ex hiftoria conftat, patri propugnato ftrenuus, et in bello fere femper victor. Vixit Cynddelw in *Povifia*, et fuit Madoci filii Maredudd, illius regionis principis, Bardus aulicus.

Gwerfyll torfoedd tew llew lladdai,
Gorfaf tarf, taerfalch fal Gwalchmai,
Gorfaran Gwrfan gorfyddai,
Gwr yn aer yn aros gwaedd fai,
Bryd Erof gryd, arf greu a ddodai,
Brwydr eurgrwydr, eurgrawn ni guddiai,
Bradog waith gwynniaith gwynnygai,
Brys briwgad, brig bragad briwai,
Brwyfc lafneu ynghreu ynghrai celanedd,
Cymminedd cymmynai,

Gwyrdd

Gwyrdd heli *Teifi* tewychai,
Gwaedlan gwyr, a llyr ai llanwai,
Gwyach rudd gorfudd goralwai,
Ar donniar gwyar gonofiai,
Gwyddfeirch tonn torrynt yn ertrai,
Gwythur naws fal traws au treifiai,
Gwyddfid *Eingl* ynghladd au trychai,
Gwyddgwn coed colled au porthai,
Gwyddwal dyfneual dyfnafai fy modd,
     Fy meddiant a gaffaei.
Colleis Arglwydd call nim collai,
Corf eurdorf, eurdal am rhoddai,
Cof cadflawdd am cawdd, a'm carai,
Car cerddawr, cerddau ai cyrchai,
Gryd wafcar, llachar, a'm llochai, .
Grym dilludd DILLUS fab ERFAI,
Greddf *Greidwyr*, a *Chywyr* a *Chai*.
Glew ddefawd glyw oefdrawd aefdrai,
Yftre hynt, waftad, weftei gwynfydig
     Gwyn ei fyd bieufei.
Gwyth efcor tra mor, tra *Menai*,
Gwlydd elfydd elwais o honai,
Tra fu OWAIN mawr ai meddai,
Medd a gwin a gwirawd fyddai,
Gwynedd wen Gwyndyd len ledpai,
Gwedi gwawr, cad fawr ai cadwai,
Pa wladwr, arwr arwyndai,
     Pa wledig a wledych arnai?

          i. e.

  " Denfas turmas in conflictu occidit leo,
  " Qui fuit inftar GWALCHMAI actis ad fugandum hoftes ,
                          " Superavit

" Superavit magnas copias Gwrfanni.

" Fuit in bello vir qui tubam expectabat,

" Similis Erof bellicofo, qui telum cruentum duxit.

" Ex bello rediens, in quo aurum nactus eft, thefaurum non recondit;

" In hoftes dolofos certans magnâ excanduit irâ;

" Haftæ in bello furiofæ erant in cadaveribus occiforum

" Et acies (gladiorum) fe invicem contriverunt.

    " Viridis aqua *Teivii* pinguis facta fuit,

" Fluxus virorum fanguinis et maris eum ripas fuperare fecit,

" Et f rubra avis aquatilis, pro magno habebat emolumento,

" Et per fluvios cruoris natabat,

" Et alti marini equi (i. e. fluctus) plangebant in littore.

" Magnanimus ille princeps eos inftar tyranni oppreffit,

" Et Anglorum cumulos in fofla truncavit.

" Sylveftres canes amiferunt opfonatorem,

" Quibus in denfis vepribus affolebat effe victus, neque meo affenfu,

    " Neque auxilio indigebat.

" Perdidi dominum prudentem, qui me non neglexit,

" Cujus corpus erat auro amictum, quique mihi aurum dedit,

" Cujus memoria (mortui) me lædit : qui me dilexit :

" Amicus enim erat Bardo, et eum appetebant carmina

" Ille qui homines in bello diffipare fecit, et cujus impetus erat violen-

    " tus me fovit,

" Cujus robur erat ineluctabile inftar Dillus filii Erfai,

" Et cujus ingenium erat fimile Greidwyr, Cywyr et Cai.

" Herois inftar haftam geffit comminutam

" Domi autem vitæ curfus erat tranquillus, hofpes enim erat munificus

    " Et ad fummam felicitatem pervenit.

---

    f Quænam fit hæc avis mihi non conftat.

                                 " Ille

" Ille victorias reportavit violentus trans æstuarium *Menai*
" Ubi terra est benigna, ex qua beneficium sum nactus:
" Donec extitit OWENUS magnus qui *Monam* possesit,
" Mulsum, vinum et *ᵉ gwirawd* bibimus.
" O *Venedotia* olim beata, Venedotorum tutamen asperu,
" Post Heroem bellicosum qui te defendet!
" Quis ex nostratibus heros in ædibus vivens magnificis,
" Quis princeps te gubernare æquo ac ille valebit ?

SED non semper in bellatorum laudes effusi erant Bardi ; sæpe
etiam principum et magnatum fata indigna lugubriter canebant. Sed
infinitum esset hæc singulatim recensere. Unum sat est adducere
exemplum, ex quo de aliis facile judicari potest. LEOLINO GRUF-
FINI filio, ultimo Cambriæ principe, juxta *Buellt* dolo sublato, dici
non potest quanto id Bardos dolore affecit. Inter quos GRUFFUDD
AP YR YNAD COCH hæc texuit admodum παθητικῶς.

Llawer llef druan, fal pan fu *Gamlan*,
Llawer deigr dros rann gwedi gronniaw,
O leas gwanas gwanar eurllaw,
O laith LLYWELYN cof dyn nim daw,
Oerfelog calon, dan fron o fraw,
Rhewydd, fal crinwydd y sy'n crinaw,
Poni welwch chwi hynt y gwynt ar glaw ?
Poni welwch chwi'r deri yn ymdaraw ?
Poni welwch chwi'r mor yn merwino'r tir ?
Poni welwch chwi'r gwir yn ymg'weiriaw ?
Poni welwch chwi'r haul yn hwylio'r awyr ?
Poni welwch chwi syr wedi syrthiaw ?

ᵉ Potius genus apud veteres Britannos.

Poni

Poni chredwch i Dduw ddyniadon ynfyd
Poni welwch chwi'r byd wedi bydiaw?
Och hyd attat di Dduw na ddaw mor tros dir
Pa beth in gedir i ohiriaw?
Nid oes le i cyrcher rhag carchar braw
Nid oes le i triger och! o'r trigaw,
Nid oes na chyngor, na chlo nag agor,
Na ffordd i efgor brwyn gyngor braw!

i. e.

" Frequens eft vox lugubris, veluti olim in *Camlan,*
" Multæ lacrymæ in genis accumulantur,
" Eo quod occidit Cambriæ fuftentaculum, et ejus dominus
    " munificus,
" Ex quo occidit Leolinus de cæteris non curo;
" Cor frigidum eft fub pectore ob horrorem,
" Et is qui prius hilaris erat, jam marcefcit.
" Nonne videtis venti et imbris curfum?
" Nonne videtis quercus in fe invicem ruentes?
" Nonne videtis mare terram vaftans?
" Nonne videtis folem ex curfu aerio dofleftentom?
" Nonne videtis aftra ex orbibus corruiffe?
" Cur Deo non creditis homines, vefani?
" Nonne videtis mundi finem adeffe?
" Exclamabo ufque ad te, o Deus, cur terram non abforbet mare,
" Et cur diutius relinquimur in angore languere?
" Nullus eft locus, quem petamus ægri,
" Nullus locus, in quo habitemus miferi,
" Nullum reftat confilium, nullum effugium,
" Nulla via, qua evitemus fatum luctuofum.

5

Floruere

FLORUERE a tempore GRUFFINI CONANI filii ad hunc LEOLINUM et multi alii Bardi infignes, inter quos eminet LLYWARCH cognomine Prydydd y Moch, qui LEOLINI Magni, noftris LLEWELYN AP JORWERTH, victorias multis celebravit odis, uti et fecere DAFYDD BENFRAS, DANIEL AP LLOSGWRN MEW, LLYWELYN FARDD AP CYWRYD.

FLORUIT eodem tempore in *Ceretia* PHYLYP BRYDYDD, qui Bardus fuit RHYS GRYG et RHYS JEUANC ex familia RHYS AP TEWDWR oriundus.

LONGUM effet fingulos recenfere ; de præftantioribus pauca prælibaffe fufficit. Cum Cambriam in fuam poteftatem redegerat EDWARDUS primus, in Bardos fæviit tyranni inftar, et multos fufpendi fecit. Quid mirum, cum ipfum LEOLINUM principem et DAVIDEM fratrem tam inhumaniter tractaverit ? Sed EDWARDUS a LEOLINO olim in fugam pulfus, noluit illi nec affeclis ignofcere. Hinc illæ lacrymæ. Bardis objiciebatur quod cives in feditionem excitarunt, id eft re vera, quod eos ad vindicandum libertatem priftinam majorum more hortarentur. Bardi enim fuere *Cambris* idem quod olim *Athenienfibus* oratores, quos ut Græciam in fervitutem redigeret, fibi tradi voluit PHILIPPUS Macedo. Regum Angliæ jufticiarii poft *Edwardum* in Cambria ejus exemplum fecuti, Bardos legibus iniquis obnoxios ubique fuftulerunt ; unde fit ut admodum fint rari ab eo tempore ufque ad annum 1400, quo, Anglorum excuffo fervitutis jugo, fub OWENI GLYNDWR aufpiciis, fe in libertatem prifcam vindicarunt Cambri. Hoc ævo multi claruere Bardi, inter quos JOLO GOCH OWENI magnificentiam et victorias ad fydera tulit. Fuit enim OWENUS Bardorum fautor et Mæcenas, et eos undiquaque ad aulam libe-

N   ralitate

ralitate provocabat. Eo tempore floruit DAFYDD AP GWILYM Bardorum longe venuſtiſſimus e *Ceretia* oriundus. Avunculum habuit LLYWELYN AP GWILYM de *Cryngae* et *Dêl Goch*, qui eum liberaliter educabat. Patronus ejus fuit IFOR HAEL de *Baſſaleg*, cujus munificentiam et magnanimitatem multis profequitur laudibus. Cum OWENI retro laberentur res, Cambros more inaudito oppreſſit HENRICUS IV. et patriæ fatum fubiere Bardi. Lege enim cautum erat ne annuam peragrationem et conventus, noſtris *Clera* et *Cymhortha*, celebrarent. Hæc fuit caufa cur multi hoc fæculo tam obfcure fcripferint: multis enim cantibus *Cywydd Brut*, i. e. *Carminis fatidici* nomen indidere; quod et fecere poſtea cum inter *Eboracenfes* et *Lancaſtrenfes* graſſaretur factio. HENRICUS V. multum a paterna remifit in Cambros fævitia. Abeo tempore longa floruit Bardorum feries, et in magnatum ædibus alebantur, ubi eorum genealogias et figna gentilitia texebant, eorumque virtutes, fcilicet magnanimitatem, hofpitalitatem et alias animi atque corporis ingenuas et honeſtas dotes debita profequebantur laude. Mos enim fuit Britannis olim, uti et nunc Cambris, ut longam majorum feriem producerent, et Bardi qui hoc munere funt functi ARWYDDFEIRDD funt appellati, et carmen texucre "parafe-
" maticum, quod cum profapia generifve ferie, etiam et παρασήμαΊα,
" id eſt infignia nobilium et generoforum defcribit ea, quæ in veſtibus
" et vexillis et hujufmodi aliis infignita confpiciuntur, quæque fiunt
" aut feruntur, ita ab iis difcreta ut nofci poſſint quorum fint, five ad
" quos pertineant, more antiquorum bene meritis tributa, et tanquam
" ornamenta laudis et gloriæ, vel ob propriam vel fuorum majorum
" virtutem comparata."—Vide JOHANNIS DAVIDIS RHESI Linguæ
Cymraecæ Inſtitutiones accuratas pag. 146. Ex quo et hæc de hujufcemodi Bardo tranſtulimus p. 303. " *Pwy bynnag a ddywetto ei*
" *fod yn Arwyddfeird l, gwybydded achoedd Brenhinoedd a Thywyſſogion, a*
" *chyfarwyddyd o'diwrth y tri Phrifardd ynys Prydain, nid amgen,*
" MYRDDIN

" Myrddin ap Morfryn, *a* Myrddin Emrys *a* Thaliesin
" Ben Beirdd." i. e. " Quicunque voluerit effe Bardus parafenia-
" ticus, neceffe eft ut fciat regum et principum ftemmata, et fit bene
" verfatus in operibus Merlini Morfrynii filii, Merlini Am-
" brosii et Taliesini fummi Bardi." Et hoc fuiffe antiquitus
Bardorum munus annotavit Giraldus Cambrensis. " Hoc mihi
" notandum videtur, quod Bardi Cambrenfes et cantores feu recitato-
" res genealogias habent prædictorum principum in libris eorum anti-
" quis et autenticis, eandemque memoriter tenent a Roderico
" Magno ufque ad Belinum Magnum, et inde ufque ad Sylvium,
" Ascanium et Æneam, et ab ea ufque ad Adam generationem
" linealiter producunt."

Non abs re fore judicavi hic monumentum vetus inferere, quod in
manufcripto Joh. Dav. Rhesi propria manu exarato inveni. Quod
quidem manufcriptum dignum eft omnino quod prelo mandetur.:
noftram enim linguam poefin, et alia vetufta monumenta adverfus
ignarum quendam calumniatorem, quorum meffem innumeram hæc
æque ac fuperior ætas tul't, ftrenue vindicat. Hic tractatus in lingua
Britannica eleganter fcriptus eft, et talium nebulonum infcitiam pro-
tervam facile retundit. Videtur vir doctiffimus hoc monumentum ex vetufto aliquo fcriptore nunc deperdito excerpfiffe. Utcunque fit, id ego ex ejus autographo hic fideliter exfcri bere curavi.
" Blethinus filius Cynvini patri in principatu " *Povifiæ*
" fucceffit. Hic templa, caftra et maneria renovari fecit, leges
" Howeli obfervavit. Inter tres principes, videlicet, Gruffi-
" num filium Conani principem *Venedotiæ*, Blethinum filium
" Cynvini principem Povisiæ, et Rhesum filium Tewdwr prin-
" cipem *Suth-walliæ* inquifitio magna fuit de armis et de regali fan-
" guine antiquorum Britonum. Quibus conquifitis in ditione fa-
" pientium

" pientium Walliæ ; repertæ fuerunt tres lineæ regales, et quindecim
" lineæ de fanguine nobilium fenatorum Britanniæ. Hic BLETHINUS
" primus omnium principum *Povifiæ*, in armis ufus eft leone rubeo
" in fulphure. Hic caftrum de *Dol y Forwyn* fundavit, et apud *Mifod*
" fepultus eft."

Sunt in iftis genealogiis multa quæ antiquario Britannico ufui effe
poffunt ; nihil enim apud noftrates vel antiquius vel magis autenti-
cum extat, et nihil quod magis noftram illuftrat et confirmat hifto-
riam. Nonnulli enim ex Bardis non folum rei poeticæ, verum etiam
hiftoricæ mentem appulerunt. Erat in monafteriis uber hiftoriarum,
genealogiarum et poefeos collectio. Bardi enim ab abbatibus maxime
fovebantur, et erant in feftis folennibus ab iis laute excepti : uti conftat ex operibus GUTTO'R GLYNN, GUTTUN OWAIN, JEUAN
DEULWYN et TUDUR ALED. Extant et nunc in nobiliorum ædibus
innumera Epicedia, quæ noftrates *Cywyddau Marwnad* nuncupavere :
fuit enim Bardi domeftici munus, cum aliquis e familia obierit, ejus
Epicedium concinnare, quod poft exequias ad cognatos fuit delatum
et coram iis a Rhapfodis quos noftrates *Datceiniaid* nominavere reci-
tatum. Inter alia quæ in defuncti honorem funt narrata, ejus gene-
alogiam memorare tenebatur, ex quibus nobilibus ortus fuerit fami-
liis, et quæ præclara fecerint ejus majores facinora. Hujufcemodi
poematum multa vidi exemplaria pulchre exarata. Ab ELIZABETHAE
Reginæ tempore nullus fuit Bardorum legitimus confeffus : unde fit
ut nil fit deinceps accurate et fecundum profodiæ regulas fcriptum :
eoufque ut jamdudum Bardorum et hiftoricorum opera (ex quibus
folis vera et genuina Britanniæ hiftoria petenda eft) in maximo fint
periculo ne funditus pereant. Quod multas ob caufas in feculo tam
docto et fagaci maxime eft deplorandum, funt quidem hoc ævo qui
hæc ftudia velint rediviva, et qui plus ipfi poffint in re poetica atque

hiftorica

hiftorica quam quos fuperior tulit ætas. Inter quos focietas *Cymmro-dorion* Londini, patriæ atque maternæ linguæ amore inftigata, inter alia laude digna inftituta, nonnulla veterum et recentiorum melioris notæ Bardorum poemata typis mandare meditatur. Opus profecto omnibus Cambris ingenuis gratiffimum et longe defideratiffimum. Optandum eft potius quam expectandum, ut ii qui habent aliquid in poefi vel hiftoria notatu dignum in privatis bibliothecis reconditum, id in vulgus emittant, aut faltem ab iis qui hujufmodi rebus operam navant perlegi permittant. Sic enim fuæ famæ et patriæ commodo melius confulent quam vermibus et muribus committere.

Ego autem in Cambriæ montibus degens a bibliothecis et mufeis procul, quod potui feci; utinam ii qui plus poffint, et materiam uberiorem funt nacti de Bardis, et cæteris Britannicæ antiquitatis requiis, meliora cudant.

F I N I S.

YCHYDIG

A W D L A U

O waith yr hen Feirdd, yn amfer TYWYSOGION CYMRU,

Wedi eu cyfieithu i'r SAESONEG;

Er mwyn dangos anfawdd ein Prydyddiaeth i wyr cywraint,
dyfgedig, anghyfiaith : â nodau byrrion, i eglurhau enwau
Dynion, a Lleoedd, a grybwyllir ynddynt; a hanes byrr o
honynt, wedi ei gafglu allan o *Drioedd Ynys Prydain*, a hen
Goffadwriaethau eraill; er dywenydd i'r oes hon, ac er adfer
ei haeddedigawl barch i'r hen famiaith *Gymraeg*, ac i'n Gwlad;
a'u dyledus glod i'w thrigolion dewrwych gynt.

'Αιεὶ τᾶτο Διὸς κύραις μέλει, αἰὲν ἀοιδοῖς
Ὑμνεῖν ἀθανάτως, ὑμνεῖν ἀγαθῶν κλέα ἀνδρῶν.

TIIEOCRITUS Idyll. xvi.

AT

RISIART MORYS, Yſwain,

Llywydd Cymdeithas y CYMMRODORION yn LLUNDAIN;

A'I FRODYR,

LEWIS MORYS o BENBRYN, yng NGHEREDIGION, Yſwain;

A

WILIAM MORYS o GAER GYBI, ym MON.

NI'bum yn hir yn myfyrio ibwy i cyflwynwn yr ychydig Awdlau ſydd yn canlyn, canys ni adwaen i neb heddyw ag ſydd yn eu dcall cyſtal â chwi, na neb chwaith ſydd yn coledd ac yn mawrhau ein Iaith mor anwylgu Frutannaidd. I mae ein Gwlad ni yn rhwyme-dig i bob un o honoch: I chwi y *Llywydd*, yn enwedig, am y goſal a gymmeraſoch yn golygu argraphiad diweddaf y *Bibl Cyſſegrlan*, er lles tragywyddol encidiau ein cydwladwyr. Ef a dâl Duw i chwi am y Gorchwyl eluſengar yma, pan i bo'r byd hwn, a'i holl fawredd a'i wychder, wedi llwyr ddiflannu. Ac i mae'r Wlad a'r Iaith yn dra rhwymedig i'r *Gaer o Benbryn*, am gaſglu cymmaint o *Hanefion*

O
ynglylcb

ynghylch ein Hynafiaid, na chlywodd y *Saefon* braidd fon erioed am
danynt. Ef a ddelwent ddilynwyr *Camden,* pei gwelynt fal i mae yn
argyhoeddi ac yn ceryddu eu beiau, a'u tuedd gwyrgam, yn bychanu
ac yn diftadlu y pethau nad ydynt yn eu deall; ac o wir wenwyn yn
taeru mai dychymmygion diweddar ydynt. Gobeithio i cawn ni
weled y tryfor mawrwerthiog yma ar gyhoedd; i beri gofteg, ac i
dorri rhwyfg y cyfryw oganwyr ein hen Hanefion.—Nid bychan o
les i mae y *Gwr o Gaer Gybi* ynteu yn ei wneuthur, trwy gafglu *Gwaith*
yr hen Feirdd godidog gynt; ac ir wyf yn cyfaddef mai o'i lyfrau ef
i cefais i y rhan fwyaf o'r odlau fydd yn canlyn. Ni fedrwn lai nâ
dywedyd hyn, am eich ewyllys da i'ch Gwlad a'ch Iaith; cynneddfau
fydd, yfywaeth, mor brin ac anaml yn yr oes hon. Ef a ddichon hyn
beri i'n Gwlad agor ei llygaid, a defnyddio yn well rhagllaw yr hen
yfgrifenadau fydd heb fyned ar goll. Ac os na wna hi hynny, i mae
yn rhaid addef i chwi eich trioedd wneuthur eich rhan yn odiaeth.
Hyn a'm hannogodd i reddi blaenffrwyth fy llafur, er nad yw ond
bychan, dan eich nodded; a gobeithio nad ydyw lwyr annheilwng i'w
gyhoeddi, ag i daw rhywun cywreiniach i ddiwygio yr hyn fydd
ammherffaith, ac i ofod allan bethau eraill godidoccach. Nid oedd
genyfi ond torri'r garw, gobeithio i daw eraill i lyfnhau a gwaftattau y
balciau. Yn ddiau ni fuafwn i yn cymmeryd yr Orcheft yma arnaf,
ond darfod edliw o'r *Saefon,* nad oes genym ddim mewn Prydyddiaeth
a dâl ei ddangos i'r byd: a bod un o drigolion yr *Uch Alban,* gwedi
cyfieithu fwrn o Waith hen Fardd; neu yn hytrach wedi addurno a
thacclu rhyw Waith diweddar, a'i ofod allan yn ei enw ef. Chwi a
wyddoch yn dda, oddiwrth Waith ein hen Feirdd awduraidd ni,
fydd etto i'w gweled, nad ydyw ddim tebygol fod y Bardd gogleddig
mor henaidd: ond nid af i i ymyrryd ag ef ym mhellach yr awron.
I mae yn ddigon genyfi roddi hyn o brawf o'n hen Feirdd ein hunain
i'r byd; ac os darfu i mi wneuthur Cyfiawnder iddynt, dyna fi wedi

cyrraedd

cyrraedd fy amcan. Pa fodd bynnag i digwyddo, i mae'n llawen genyf gael odfa i dyftiolaethu, fy mod yn mawrygu yn ddirfawr eich Cariad a'ch traferch chwi at eich Gwlad a'ch Iaith ; yn yr hyn i damunwn, yn ol fy ngallu, eich canlyn ; a datcan, yngwydd yr holl fyd, fy mod, frodyr haeddbarch,

Eich Gwafanaethwr rhwymedig, goftyngeiddiaf,

E V A N E V A N S.

A T Y

A T Y.

C Y M R Y.

PAN welais fod un o *Yſgodogion Ucheldir Alban*, ac hefyd *Sais* dyſgedig, wedi cyfieithu Gwaith eu hen Feirdd i'r *Saeſoneg* ; mi a dybygais mai nid gweddus i ni, y *Cymry*, y rhai ſydd genym Gerddi awduraidd, gorhenaidd, o'r einom, fod yn llwyr ddiymdro yn y cyngaws hwnnw : o herwydd, hyd i gwn i, dyna'r unig ragorgamp celfyddyd a adawodd ein hynafiaid ini, ſydd heb ei cholli. I mae *Gwaith y Derwyddon*, od oedd dim gwiwgof ganddynt wedi ei yſgrifennu, wedi myned ar ddifancoll ; ac nid oes dim wedi dyfod i'n hoes ni oddiwrthynt, ond y Brydyddiaeth yn unig. I mae ein hen *Fuſic* wedi ei llwyr ebargofio : nid yw'r cyweiriau Cwynſanus ſydd genym yr awron ond dychymmygion diweddar, pan oedd y *Cymry* yn griddſan tan iau galed y *Saeſon*. Am Gelfyddydau eraill, od oedd dim mewn perffeithrwydd, i mae gwedi ei lwyr golli. Nid oes genym ddim Hanes am ein Hynafiaid o'n hawduron ein hunain, ond oddiwrth y Beirdd yn unig, o flaen *Gildas ap Caw* ; yr hwn ſydd yn ein goganu, ac yn ein llurginio, yn hytrach nag yſgrifennu cywir Hanes am danom ; ond ſo wyr Haneſyddion yr achos : heblaw hyn, i mae ei waith ef wedi myned drwy ddwylo'r *Meneich* ; Gwyr a ſedrai yn dda ddigon, dylino pob peth i'w dibenion eu hunain.—Y Beirdd fal i tyſtia *Giraldus* Arch-diacon *Brycheiniog*, oeddynt yn cadw Achau y Brenhinoedd, ac yn coffau eu gweithredoedd ardderchog ; ac oddiwrthynt hwy yn ddiammau i deryw i *Dyſilio* ſab *Brochwel Yſgythreg*, tywyſog

tywyfog *Powys*, yfgrifennu'r *Hanes* fydd yr awron yn myned tan enw
BRUT Y BRENHINOEDD, yr hwn a ddarfu i *Galfrid ap Arthur*, o
Aber Mynwy, ei gyfieithu o Iaith *Llydaw* i'r *Lladin*, ac oddiyno yn
Gymraeg; fel i mae ef ei hunan yn cyfaddef, mewn amryw hen go-
piau ar femrwn, fydd etto i'w gweled yng Nghymru; ond yfywaeth,
e ddarfu iddo chwanegu amryw chwedlau at hanes *Tyfilio*; *Flamines*
ac *Archiflamines*, a phrophwydoliaeth *Myrddin Emrys*, a phethau
craill a fuafai harddach eu gadael heibio. Ped fuafai yn dilyn y
Beirdd, e fuafai genym gywirach Hanes nag fydd genym yrawron; ond
fel ag i mae, ni haeddai yn gwbl mor gogan i mae'r *Saefon*, o amfer
Camden, yn ei rhoi iddi; o herwydd i mae *Nennius*, yr hwn a yfgri-
fennodd drychant o flynyddoedd o'i flaen, yn rhoddi yr un Hanes am
ein Dechreuad. Ir wyf yn amcanu, os Duw a rydd im'hoedl ac
iechyd, ofod allan yr awdur hwn a nedau helaeth arno, gyd ag
amddiffyniad o'r Hanes; o herwydd efe yw'r Hanefydd hynaf a
feddwn yn *Lladin*, oddigerth y *Gildas* uchod, yr hwn nid yw deilwng
ei gyfrif yn Hanefydd; o herwydd nid dyna ei gyngyd na'i fympwy,
yn ei *Epiftolæ de excidio Britanniæ*. Ir wyf yn methu a chaffael copi
iawn o *Nennius*, ac ir wyf yn meddwl nad oes un yng Nghymru a
dâl ddim, ond yn *Hengwrt*: da iawn er lles y Wlad a Hanefyddion
Prydain, i gwnai ei Berchennog adael i ryw wr dyfgedig ei gymhâru.
I mae genyfi ddau gopi, ond i maent yn drâ aminherffaith; felly
hefyd i mae'r rhai printiedig, o eiddo'r Dr. *Gale* a *Bertram*. Ni
wiw i *Sais*, na neb dieithr, bydded mor ddyfgedig ag i mynno, oni
ddeall ef *Gymraeg* yn iawn, ac oni chaiff hefyd weled ein hen yfgrifenadau a'n Beirdd ni, gyteam â'r fath waith. Nid yw *Camden*, er
dyfgedicced, diwytted, a manyled gwr ydoedd, ond ymleferydd am
lawer o bethau yn ei *Britannia*; a hynny yn unig, o achos nad oedd
yn medru yr iaith yn well. A grefyn yw, nad oedd y *Saefon*, y rhai
oeddynt yn ddiau (rai o naddunt) yn chwilio pethau yn dêg, ac yn
ddiduedd dros ben, y cyfryw ag ydoedd *Leland*, *Ufher*, a *Selden*, yn

deall

dèall ein Iaith, a medru gwneuthur defnydd o'n hen Lyfrau : o herwydd hyn, nid oeddynt, er cymmaint eu dyfg a'u dawn, ddim i'w cyffelybu ag *Wmffre Llwyd* o *Ddinbych*, a *Rhobert Fychan* o'r *Hengwrt*, fel i mae eu·gwaith yn eglur ddangos.   Ac yn ddiau, mae yn ammhofibl i undyn, bydded mor gywreinied ag i mynno, wneuthur dim â ffrwyth ynddo, heb gaffael gweled yr hen yfgrifenadau, fydd yn gadwedig yn llyfr-gelloedd y boneddigion yng *Nghymru* ; yn enwedig yn *Hengwrt*, a *Llan Fordaf*. Myfi a welais, ac a gefais fenthyg amryw lyfrau o waith llaw, yn llyfrgrawn yr anrhydeddus *Robert Davies*, yfg^r. o *Lannerch* yn fwydd *Ddinbych* ; a Syr *Roger Moflyn* yng *Ngloddaith*, feneddwr dros Swydd *Fflint* ; a chan yr anrhydeddus *Wiliam Fychan*, yfg^r. o *Gors y Gedol*, feneddwr dros fwydd *Feirionydd* ; yr hyn ni fedraf lai nâ'i fynegi yma yngwydd y byd, er coffau eu Cymmwynas a'u hewyllys da i'n Gwlad a'n Iaith, ac i minnau hefyd ; yn ol arfer canmoladwy, a haelioni yr hen *Frython* gynt.

OND i ddyfod weithion at y Bèirdd, y rhai a adawfom ar ol.   Ef a ddarfu imi gyfieithu ychydig odlau o'u Gwaith, trwy annogaeth Gwyr dyfgedig o *Loegr* ; ac mi a ewyllyfiwn wneuthur o honof hynny er clod iddynt ; ond i mae yn rhaid im' adael hynny ym marn y darllenyddion : ac nid oes genyfi ddim i'w ddywedyd, os drwg yw'r cyfieithiad, nad arnaf i yn llwyr i mae'r bai yn fefyll ; o herwydd i maent y Beirdd yn ddiammau yn orcheftol odiaeth ; ond i mae'n rhaid addef hefyd eu bod yn anhawdd afrifed eu deongli, o herwydd eu bod yn llawn o eiriau fydd yr awron wedi myned ar gyfrgoll : ac nid ydynt wedi eu heglurhau mewn un Geiriadur argraphedig nac yfgrifenedig a welais i.   Ir oedd yr Athraw hynod o *Fallwyd*, yr hwn a aftudiodd yr Iaith,. er lles cyffredin y wlad, dros holl ddyddiau ei einioes, yn methu eu deongli. Ac ni wnaeth y dyfgedig Mr. *Edward Llwyd* o'r *Mufæum*, gamp yn y byd yn y perwyl yma, er ei fod yn gydnabyddus â holl geinciau prifiaith *Prydain*. Ac yn ddiau o'r

2   achos

achos yma, nid oedd genyfi ddim ond ynibalfalu am yſtyr a
ſynwyr y Beirdd, mewn llawer man, ·oddiwrth flaen ac ol. Ir
wyf yn rhyfeddu'n ddirfawr am rai o'r *Cymry* ſydd yn haeru fod
·gwaith *Talieſin*, ai gydoeſuid *Aneurin Gwawdrydd*, *Llywarch Hen*,
a *Merddin Wyllt*, yn hawdd eu deall. Yn ddiau nid wyf i yn
·deall mo honynt, ac i mae'r rhai dyſgediccaf yn yr Iaith, y to
heddyw, yn addeſ yr un peth. I mae'r Beirdd, hir oeſoedd gwedi hynny, ſeſ ar ol dyfodiad ·*Gwilym Faſdardd*, hyd farwolaeth *Llywelyn ap*
·*Gruffydd*, yn dywyll iawn; fal i gellwch weled oddiwrth yr odlau ſydd
yn canlyn. Hyn a barodd i mi beidio â chyfieithu chwaneg o honynt
y tro yma, rhag oſn imi, trwy ſy anwybedaeth, wneuthur cam â
hwynt. ·Ond gan i'r *Saeſon* daeru, na feddwn ddim mewn pry-
·dyddiaeth a dâl ei ddangos; mi a wnaethum fy ngorau er cyfieithu y
Caſgliad bychan yma, i ſwrw heibio, os yw beſiibl, y gogan hwnnw:
ac yn ·ddiau, os na lwyddodd genyf wneuthur hynny, i mae yn
rhaid i'r Beirdd, a'm Cydwladwyr, ſaddeu imi; a gobeithio i derbyn-
iant fy ewyllys da, herwydd na ddichon neb wneuthur ond a allo.
—Heblaw hyn oll, i mae hyn o waith yn dyfod i'r byd, mewn amſer anghyfaddas i ymddangos mewn dim prydſerthwch; o herwydd i
mae un o drigolion yr *Uch Alban*, gwedi goſod allan ddau lyfr o
Waith *Offian*; hen Fardd, meddai ef, cyn dyfod Criſtianogaeth i'w
plith. Ac i mae'r llyfrau hyn mewn rhagorbarch gan foneddigion
dyſgedig y *Saeſon*. A rhaid addeſ eu bod wedi eu cyfieithu yn odidog:
ond i mae arnaſi ofn, wedi'r cwbl, fod yr *Yſgodog* yn bwrw hug ar
lygaid dynion, ac nad ydynt mor hen ag i mae ef yn taeru eu bod.
I mae'r *Gwyddelod* yn arddelw *Offian* megis un o'u Cydwladwyr
hwynt; ac i mae amryw bethau yn y Cerddi a gyhoeddwyd yn ei
enw, yn dangos, yn fy nhyb i, oes ddiweddarach nag i mae'r cyſi-
eithydd yn ſon am dani; yn enwedig dyfodiad Gwyr *Llychlyn* i'r
Iwerddon, yr hyn ni ddigwyddodd, meddai Haneſyddion yr *Iwerddon*,
cyn y flwyddyn 760. Ac ni ddaeth yr *Yſgodogion* chwaith i ſeſydlu yn
yr *Alban*, o flaen *Fergus Mec Eirs*, ynghylch y flwyddyn 503; fal i
mae

*mae *Wiliam Llwyd*, Efgob *Caer Wrangon*, wedi ei brofi yn ddiwrthadl, yn ei lyfr ynghylch llywodraeth eglwyfig. Ond pei canniatteid eu bod hwy yno cyn hynny, ni fyddai hynny ronyn nes i brofi *Offian* mor hyned ag i dywedir ei fod. O herwydd ped fuafai, Pa fodd i mae ei gyfieithydd yn medru ei ddeongli mor hyfedr? I mae gwaith ein Beirdd ni, fydd gant o flynyddoedd ar ol hynny, tu hwnt i ddeall y Gwyr cywreiniaf a medrufaf yn yr hen *Frutaniaith*. Pwy o honom ni a gymmerai'r *Gododin*, Gwaith *Aneurin Gwawdrydd*, Fychdeyrn Beirdd, a'i gyfieithu mor llathraidd ag i gwnaeth cyfieithydd *Ffingal* a *Themora*? Ir wyfi yn meddwl nad oes neb a ryfygei gymmeryd y fath orcheft arno. Prin iawn i medrais i ddeongli rhai pennillion o hono yma a thraw, y rhai a ellwch eu gweled yn y traethawd *Lladin* ynghylch y Beirdd. A grefyn yw ei fod mor dywyll, o herwydd, hyd ir wyf i yn ei ddeall, Gwaith godidog ydyw. Yr un peth a ellir ei ddywedyd am *Daliefin* Ben Beirdd, nid oes neb heddyw, hyd i gwn i, a fedr gyfieithu yn iawn un o'i Awdlau na'i Orchanau. Myfi a wn fod amryw Frudiau ar hyd y wlad, wedi eu tadogi ar *Daliefin* a *Myrddin*; ond nid ydynt ond dychymygion diweddar, gwedi eu ffurfeiddio ar ol marwolaeth *Llywelyn ap Gruffydd*. Yn enwedig yn amferoedd terfyfglyd *Owain Glyndwr*, a'r ymdrech rhwng pleidiau *Efrog* a *Lancafter*. I mae hefyd eraill, gwedi eu lluniaethu gan y Meneich, i atteb eu dibenion hwythau; ond i mae'r rhain oll yn hawdd eu gwahanu oddiwrth awduraidd waith *Taliefin*, wrth yr Iaith.—I mae yn ddiammau genyf, fod y Bardd yma yn odidog yn ei amfer. Ir oedd yn gydnabyddus ag athrawiaeth y *Derwyddon* am y μεἰεμψύχωσις, a'r Daroganau, y rhai oeddynt yn ddiammau weddillion o'r Credo paganaidd; caıys nid yw daroganu ddim arall ond mynegi pethau i ddyfod, oddiwrth y *Ddar*, yr hon ir oeddynt y *Derwyddon* yn ei pherchi yn fawr iawn. A chan ei fod ef yn wr llys, ac yn byw yn yr oes anwybodus honno, ir oedd yr hyn a ddywedai yn cael ei

P   dderbyn

dderbyn a'i roefawu gan y gwerinos, megis ped fuafai wir broffwyd? A hynny a ellir ei ddywedyd hefyd am *Ferddin Emrys*, a'i broffwyd-oliaeth. Mor anhawdd yw tynnu ofergoelion eu Hynafiaid, oddiwrth un Wlad neu Genedl!

E DDICHON rhai o honoch yfgatfydd ofyn, Pâham na buafwn yn cyficithu rhai o'r Beirdd godidog diweddar, a yfgrifenafant wedi diwygio yr hen gynghanedd? I'r rhain ir wyf yn atteb, fod y Beirdd yn amfer y Tywyfogion yn fwy ardderchog a mawryddig yn eu Gwaith; ac ir oeddynt eu hunain, rai o naddunt, yn Dywyfogion, ac yn Wyr dyledogion; yn enwedig, *Owain Cyfeiliog*, Tywyfog *Powys*; a *Hywel ap Owain Gwynedd*, Bardd a rhyfelwr godidog: ac felly ir oeddynt yn fwy penigamp nâ'r Beirdd diweddar, o ran eu teftunau. Canys ir oedd y Beirdd diweddar, fel i mae *Sion Dafydd Rhys* yn achwyn arnynt, yn gwen-ieithio i'r Gwyr mawr, ac yn dywedyd eelwydd ar eu cân; ac yn haeru iddynt dorri ceftyll, lladd a llofgi, pryd ir oeddynt, eb ef, yn cyfgu yn eu gwelyau, heb ddim mo'r fath feddwl nac amcan ganddynt: Eithr yn amfer y Tywyfogion, o'r gwrthwyneb; ir oedd y Beirdd yn dyftion o ddewredd a mawfrydigrwydd eu Tywyfogion; ac ir oeddynt eu hunain yn filwyr glewion. Ir oedd *Meilir Brydydd* yn gennad dros *Ruffydd ap Cynan* at Frenin *Llocgr*; ac ir oedd *Gwalchmai*, ei fab, yn Flaenor cad ynghyffinydd *Llocgr* a *Chymru*; fel i maent ill dau yn tyftiolaethu yn eu Cerddi. Heblaw hyn, ir oedd y Tywyf-ogion yma yn fuddugawl yn eu rhyfeloedd a'r *Saefon*, ac ir oedd hynny yn peri i'r Beirdd ymorcheftu, i dragywyddoli eu gweithred-oedd ardderchog; ac i foli eu gwroldeb, mewn achos mor glodfawr ag amddiffyn eu Gwlad a'u Rhyddid, yn erbyn Eftron genedl, a'u difuddiafei o Dreftadaeth eu Hynafiaid. Ir oedd y rhain yn ddiau yn Deftunau gwiw i Feirdd ganu arnynt, ac yn fodd cymmwys i beri i'w Deiliaid eu perchi a'u hanrhydeddu; Canys ir oedd y cerddi godi-dog yma yn cael eu datgan gyda'r Delyn, mewn Cyweiriau cyfaddas,

mewn

mewn Gwleddau yn Llys y Tywyſog, ac yn Neuaddau y Pende-
figion a'r Uchelwyr. I mae *Giraldus* yn dywedyd, fod y *Cymry* mor
ddrud a milwraidd yn ei amſer ef, ag na ruſynt ymladd yn noeth ac
yn ddiarſog, a'r rhai arſog, llurigog ; a'r Pedydd yn erbyn y Marchiog-
ion. Yn ddiau, nid oedd un modd a ellid ei ddychymmygu well,
i gynnal yr yſpryd dihiſarch yma yn ein Hynaſiaid, na chael eu moli
gan y Beirdd. Ac e wyddai'r *Saeſon* hynny yn dda ddigon ; Canys ar
ol daroſtwng *Cymru* tan eu llywodraeth, e ddarfu iddynt ddihenyddu'r
Beirdd trwy'r holl Wlad. I mae llyſrau yſtatud *Lloegr*, yn llawn o
Gyfreithiau creulon i'w herbyn, ac yn gwaraſun yn gaeth iddynt
ymarſer o'u hen Ddefodau, o Glera a chymhortha. Yn amſer *Owain
Glyndwr*, i cawſant ychydig ſcibiant a chynhwyſiad i ganu ; ond
gwedi hynny, hyd ddyſodiad *Harri'r Seithſed*, ir oeddynt tan gwm-
mwl. Gwedi iddo ef ddyſod i Lywodraethu, ac yn amſer ei ſab
Harri'r Wythſed, a'r Frenhines *Eliſabeth*, y rhai a hanoeddynt o waed
Cymreig, i cawſant gynhwyſiadau i gynnal Eiſteddſodau : ond ni
pharhaodd hynny ond ennyd fechan, o herwydd Bonedd *Cymru* a
ymroiſant i fod yn *Saeſon*, fel i maent yn parhau gan mwyaf hyd y
dydd heddyw.

Ond i mae rhai yn yr oes yma yn chwenychu eu cadw a'u coledd,
er mwyn eu hiaith ddigymmyſg, ac er mwyn gwell gwybodaeth o
foeſau ac anſawdd ein Hynaſiaid ; ac er mwyn eu teilyngdod eu hunain ; o herwydd i mae yn rhai o'u Hawdlau a'u Cywyddau, ymadrodd-
ion mor gywraint a naturiol ag ſydd ym Mhrydyddion *Groeg* a
Rhuſain ; mal i gwyr y ſawl a'u deallant yn dda.—Ymyſg eraill, i
mae Cymdeithas y *Cymmrodorion*, yn *Llundain*, yn rhoddi mowrbarch
iddynt ; ac yn chwenychu cadw cynniſer o'u hen yſgriſenadau ag ſydd
heb ſyned ar goll. A da i gwneynt Foneddigion *Cymru*, ped ymo-
ralwent am argraphu y pethau mwyaf hynod a gwiwgof mewn Pry-

dyddiaeth,

dyddiaeth, Hanefion, ac eraill hen Goffadwriaethau; o herwydd 'i
maent beunydd yn cael eu difrodi, gan y fawl ni wyddant ddim·
gwell. Hyn, er lles ein Gwlad a'n Iaith, yw gwir a diffuant dda-
muniad.

　　Eich goftyngedig wafanaethwr, a'ch ewyllyfiwr da, .

　　　　　　　　　　　　　E V A N E V A N S.

　　　　　　　　　　　　　　　　　　　H I R L A S

I.

HIRLAS OWEIN.

Owein Cyfeiliog e hun ai cant.

GWAWR pan ddwyre gawr a ddoded,
Galon yn anfon anfudd dynged,
Geleurudd ein gwyr gwedi lludded trwm,
Tremit gofwy mur *Maelawr Drefred.*

Deon a yrrais dygyhyffed,
Diarfwyd a'r frwydr arfau goched,
A rygoddwy glew gogeled rhagddaw,
Gnawd yw oi ddygnaw ddefnydd codded!

Dywallaw di feneftr gan foddhäed,
Y Corn yn llaw *Rhys* yn llys llyw ced,
Llys *Owain* ar braidd yt ryborthed erioed,
Porth mil a glywi pyrth egored.

Meneftr am gorthaw, nam adawed
Eftyn y Corn er cyd yfed,
Hiraethlawn am llyw lliw ton nawfed,
Hirlas i arwydd aur i dudded :

A dyddwg

A dyddwg o fragawd wirawd orgred,
Ar llaw *Wgan* draws dros i weithred,
Canawon *Goronwy*, gwrdd gynnired gwyth,
Canawon hydwyth, hydr eu gweithred :
Gwyr a obryn tal ymhob caled,
Gwyr yngawr gwerthfawr gwrdd ymwared,
Bugelydd *Hafren* balch eu clywed,
Bugunat cyrn medd mawr a wna neued.

Dywallaw di'r corn argynfelyn,
Anrhydeddus, feddw, o fedd gorewyn,
Ac o'r mynni hoedl hyd un blwyddyn,
Na ddidawl i barch, can nid perthyn,
A dyddwc i *Ruffudd* waywruddelyn,
Gwin a gwydr goleu yn ei gylchyn,
Dragon *Arwyftli*, arwyftl terfyn,
Dragon *Owain* hael o hil *Cynfyn*,
Dragon iw dechreu, ac niw dychryn cat,
Cyflafan argrat cymyw erlyn.
Cetwyr ydd aethant er clod obryn :
Cyfeddon, arfawc, arfau *Edwyn*,
Talaffant i medd mal gwyr *Belyn* gynt,
Teg i hydrefynt tra fo undyn.

Dywallaw di'r corn, canys amcan cenmyf,
Ydd ymgyrryw glyw gloyw ymddiddan,
Ar llaw ddehau ein llyw gyflafan,
Lluch y dan yfgwyd yfgawn lydan,
Ar llaw *Ednyfet* llawr diogan lew,
Ergyrwayw trylew, trei i darian.

Terfyfc

Terfyfc ddyffyfc ddeu ddiofn anian,
Torrynt torredwynt uch teg adfan,
Telcirw ynghyngrein ynghyfran brwydr,
Tal yfgwyd eurgrwydr torrynt yn fuan :
Tryliw eu pelycr gwedi penwan,
Trylwyn yn amwyn amwiw *Garthan*.
Cigleu ym *Maclawr* gawr fawr fuan,
A garw ddifgyrr gwyr, a gwyth erwan,
Ac ymgynnull am drull am dramwyan,
Tal i bu ym *Mangor* am ongyr dân :
I an wnaeth dau deyrn uch cyrn cyfrdan,
Pan fu gyfeddach *Forach Forfran*.

Dywallaw di'r corn, canys myfyr gennyf,
Men ydd amygant medd a'n tymmyr,
Selyf diarfwyt Orfaf *Gwygyr*,
Gogelet ai cawdd calon eryr !
Ac unmab *Madawc*, enwawg *Dudur* hael,
Hawl bleiddiad, lleiddiad, lluch ar yfgyr,
Deu arwreidd, deu lew, yn eu Cyngyr,
Deu arial dywal dau fab *Ynyr*,
Dau rydd yn nycd cad eu Cyfergyr,
Cyfargor diachor camp diachyr,
Arfod llewod gwrdd, gwrddwan cadwyr,
Aer gunieid, lunieid, coch eu hongyr,
Treis erwyr yn ffwyr ffaw ehegyr,
Trei eu dwy aefawr dan un yftyr,
Gorfu gwynt gwaeddfan uch glan glasfyr,
Gorddwy clau tonnau *Talgarth* yftyr.

Dywallaw

Dywallaw di feneftr na fyn angau,
Corn can anrhydedd ynghyfeddau,
Hirlas buelin, breint uchel hen ariant,
Ai gortho nid gorthenau :
A dyddwg i *Dudur*, eryr aerau,
Gwirawd gyffefin o'r gwin gwinau,
Oni ddaw i mewn o'r medd gorau oll,
Gwirawd o ban, dy ben faddau,
Ar llaw *Foreiddig*, llochiad cerddau.
Cerddyn hyn i glod cyn oer adnau,
Dieithr frodyr fryd ucheldau,
Diarchar arial a dan dalau,
Cedwyr am gorug gwafanaethau,
Nid ym hyn dihyll nam hen deheu
Cynnifieid, gyrthieid, fleinieid, fleiddiau,
Cynfaran creulawn creulyd ferau,
Glew glyw *Mochnannwys* o *Bowys* beu :
O glew gwnedd arnaddunt deu,
Achubieit pob rheid, rhudd eu harfeu :
Echedwynt rhag terfyfc eu terfynau,
Moliant yw eu rhann y rhei gwynnau;
Marwnad fu neud mi newid y ddau !
O chan Grift mor drift wyf o'r anaeleu !
O goll *Moreiddig* mawr ei eiffieu.

Dywallaw di'r corn can nim puchant,
Hirlas yn llawen yn llaw *Forgant*,
Gwr a ddyly gwawd gwahan foliant,
Gwenwyn y addwyn, gwan edrywant,

2

Areglydd defnydd dioddefiant llafn, .
Llyfn i deutu llym ei hamgant.

Dywallaw di feneftr o leftr Ariant,
Celennyg edmyg, can urdduniant,
Ar llawr *Gwoftin* fawr gwelais irdant,
Ardwy *Goronwy* oedd gweith i gant,
Cedwyr cyfarfaeth ydd ymwnaethant,
Cad ymerbyniei₁, eneid dichwant,
Cyfarfu yfgwn ac yfgarant aer,
Llas aer, llofget maer ger mor lliant:
Mwynfawr o garcharawr a gyrchaffant,
Meurig fab Gruffydd grym ddarogant,
Neud oedd gochwys pawb pan atgorfant,
Neud oedd lawn o heul hirfryn a phant.

Dywallaw di'r corn ir cynnifieid,
Canawon *Owain*, cyngrein, cydneid,
Wynt a ddyrllyddant yn lle honneid,
Glud men ydd ant gloyw heyrn ar neid :
Madawc a *Meilir* gwyr gorddyfneid treis,
Tros gyferwyr gyferbynieid :
Tariannogion torf, terfyfc ddyfgeid,
Trinheion faon, traws ardwyeid.
. Ciglau am dal medd myned dreig *Cattraeth*,
Cywir eu harvaeth, arfau lliweid,
Gofgordd Fynyddawc am eu cyfgeid,
Cawffant y hadrawdd cas flawdd flaenieid ;
Ni wnaeth a wnaeth fynghedwyr ynghalet *Faelor*,
Ðillwng Carcharor dulleft foleid.

Q   Dywallaw

Dywallaw di feneſtr fedd hidlaid, melus,
Ergyrwayw gwrys gochwys yn rhcid,
O gyrn buelin balch oreuraid,
Yr gobryn gobrwyau henaid ;
O'r gynnifer anhun a borth cynnieid
Nis gwyr namyn Duw ac ai dywaid.

Gwr ni dal ni dwng, ni bydd wrth wir,
Daniel dreig cannerth, mor ferth hewir,
Meneſtr mawr a gweith yd ioleithir
Gwyr ni oleith lleith, oni llochir,
Meneſtr medd ancwyn a'n cydroddir,
Gwrdd-dan gloyw, goleu, gwrddloyw babir
Meneſtr gwelud dy gwyth yn Llidwm dir
Y gwyr a barchaf wynt a berchir.
Meneſtr gwelud dy galchdoed Cyngrein,
Ynghylchyn *Owain* gylchwy enwir,
Pan breiddwyd Cawres, taerwres trwy dir,
Preidd oſtwng orflwng a orſolir,
Meneſtr nam didawl, nim didolir,
Boed ym mharadwys in cynhwyſir,
Can pen teyrnedd, poed hir eu trwydded,
Yn i mae gweled gwaranred gwir.

AMEN.

A W D L

II.

A   W   D   L

I Fyfanwy Feehan o Gaftell Dinas Bran.

NEUD wyf ddihunwyf, hoen Creirwy hoywdeg,
    Am hudodd mal Garwy,
O fan or byd rwymgwyd rwy,
O fynor gaer Fyfanwy.

Trymmaf yw Cariad tramwy, hoen eurnef,
    Hyn arnaf dy faccwy, .
Dy far feinwar Fyfanwy,
Ar ath gar ni fu far fwy.

Gofyn ni allawdd namyn gofwy cur,
    Dyn mewn cariad fwy fwy,
Fynawg eirian Fyfanwy,
Fuchudd ael fun hael fyw'n hwy.

Eurais wawd ddidlawd, ddadl rwy adncuboen,
    Adnabod Myfanwy,
Poen ath gar afar ofwy,
Poen brwyn ei ryddwyn i ddwy.

Gorwydd,

Gorwydd, cyrch ebrwydd, ceirch ebran addas,
  Dwg driftwas, dig Dryftan,
Llwrw buoft, farch llary buan,
Lle arlloes fre eurllys Fran.

Gwn beunydd herwydd herw amcan, ddilyd
  Ddelw berw Cafwennan :
Golwg, deddf amlwg diddan,
  Gwelw, freich fras brenhinblas Bran.

Gyrrais a llidiais farch bronn llydan, hoyw,
  Er hoen blodau firian :
Gyrrawd ofal yr Alban,
Garrhir braifc ucheldir Bran.

Lluniais wawd, ddefawd ddifan, traul ofer,
  Nid trwy lafur bychan :
Lliw ciry cynnar pen Aran,   -
Lloer bryd, lwys fryd o lys Fran.

Mireinwawr Drefawr dra fo brad im dwyn,
Gwarando fy nghwyn, frwyn freuddwydiad,
Mau glwyf a mowrnwyf murniad, huno heb
Gwrtheb teg atteb tuac attad
Mi dy fardd digardd, dygn gyftuddiad Rhun,
Gyfun laes wannllan ith lys winllad.
Mynnu ddwyf dracthu heb druthiad na gwyd
Wrthyd haul gymmryd, gamre wafdad.
Mynnud hoyw fun loyw oleuad gwledydd,
  Glodrydd, gain gynnydd, nid gan gennad,

Maint

Maint anhun haelfun hwylfad, em cyfoeth
Ddoeth, fain oleugoeth, fy nau lygad,
Medron boen goroen nid digarad was,
Heb ras, mau drachas om edrychiad.
Magwyr murwydr hydr, hydreiddiad lwyfle,
Mygrwedd haul fore eurne arnad.
Megais llwyr gludais llawer gwlad, yn ddwys,
Dy glod lwys, cynnwys pob datceiniad,
Mal hy oedd ymmy, am wyl gariad graen,
Myfanwy hoen blaen eiry gaen gawad.
Meddwl ferchawl, hawl, lliw ton hwyliad welw,
Arddelw dygynnelw heb dy gynheiliad.
Modd trift im gwnaeth Crift croefdog neirthiad llwyr,
Wanwyr oi fynwyr drwy lud fenniad.
Murn boen a mi om anynad hawl,
Serchawl eneidiawl un fynediad.
Mul i bwriais, trais tros ddirnad Duw gwyn,
Tremyn ar ddillyn porphor ddillad.
Megis ti ferch rhi, rhoddiad gynmyrredd,
Mwyfwy anrhydedd, wledd wledychiad.
Marw na byw, nwyf glyw gloyw luniad cyngaws,
Hoednaws nid anaws im am danad.
Meddwl ofeiliaint braint braidd im gad llefmair,
I gael yr eilgair wrth offeiriad.
Mafw imi brofi, brif draethiad a wnawn,
Lle nim rhoddi iawn, ne gwawn, na gwad.
Mefur cawdd anawdd i ynad eglur,
Adrawdd fy nolur ddwyfgur ddyfgiad.
Modd nad gwiw, lliw lleuad rhianedd,
Nam gwedd hud garedd, nam hoed girad.

4   Meinir

Meinir nith borthir, gwn borthiad poenau,
Yn nenn hoen blodau blawd yfpyddad.
Medraift, aur delaift adeilad gwawd,
Im nychdawd ddifrawd ddyfrys golliad.
Meddylia oth ra ath rad, ith brydydd
Talu y carydd Duw dofydd dad.
Prydydd wyf, tros glwyf, trais glud, poen gwaneg,
    Iaith laefdeg ith lwyfdud :
Fynawg riain fain funud :
    Fun arlludd hun eirllwydd hud.
Im neud glud, dy hud hydr, riain wanlleddf,
    O'r wenllys ger Dinbrain :
Aml yw gwawd gynnefawd gain,
Om araith ith dwf mirain.

Howel ap Einion Lygliw ai cant.

A W D L

III.

A　W　D　L

A gant Dafydd Benfras, i Lewelyn fab Jorwerth.

GWR a wnaeth llewych o'r gorllewin,
　　Haul a lloer addoer, addef ieffin,
Am gwnel, radd uchel, rwyf cyfychwin,
Cyflawn awen, awydd *Fyrddin*,
I ganu moliant mal *Aneurin* gynt,
　　Dydd i cant *Ododin*.
I foli gwyndawd *Gwyndyd* werin,
Gwynedd bendefig, ffynnedig ffin,
Gwanas deyrnas, deg cywrennin,
Gwreidd, teyrneidd, taer ymrwydrin,
Gwrawl ei fflamdo am fro Freiddin.
Er pan orau Duw dyn gyffefin,
Ni wnaeth ei gyftal traws arial trin.
Gorug *Llywelyn*, orllin teyrnedd,
Ar y brenhinedd braw a gorddin
Pan fu yn ymbrofi a brenin *Lloegyr*,
　　Yn llygru fwydd *Erbin*.
Oedd breifc, weifc ei fyddin,
Oedd brwyfc rwyfc rhag y godorin,
Oedd balch gwalch, golchiad ei laïn,

　　　　　　　　　　　　　　Oedd

Oedd beilch gweilch, gweled ei werin,
Oedd clywed cleddyfau finfin,
Oedd clybod clwyf ymhob elin,
Oedd briw rhiw yn nhrabludd odrin,
Oedd braw faw *Saefon* clawdd y *Cnwccin*,
Oedd bwlch llafn yn llaw gynnefin,
Oedd gwaedlyd pennau, gwedi gwaedlin rhwy,
     Yn rhedeg am ddeulin.
Llywelyn, ein llyw cyffredin,
Llywiawdr berth hyd *Borth Yfgewin*,
Ni ryfu gyftal *Gwftennin* ag ef,
     I gyfair pob gorllin.
Mi im byw be byddwn ddewin,
Ym marddair, ym mawrddawn gyffefin,
Adrawdd ei ddaed aerdrin ni allwn,
     Ni allai *Daliefin*.
Cyn adaw y byd gyd gyfrin,
Gan hoedyl hir ar dir daierin,
Cyn dyfnfedd efcyrnwedd yfcrin,
Cyn daear dyfnlas, arleflin,
Gwr a wnaeth o'r dwfr y gwin,
Gan fodd Duw a diwedd gwirin,
Nog a wnaethpwyd trais anwyd trin,
Ymhrefent ymhryfur orllin :
Ni warthäer hael am werthefin nos,
     A nawdd faint boed cyfrin.

C A N U

C A N U

*I Lywelyn fab Iorwerth. Einiawn fab Gwgawn ai
cant.*

CYFARCHAF o'm naf, am nefawl Arglwydd,
Criſt Celi culwydd, cwl i ddidawl,
Celfydd leferydd o le gweddawl,
Celfyddydau mau ni fo marwawl:
I brofi pob peth o bregeth *Bawl*,
I foli fy rhi, rhwyf angerddaw!,
Rhyfel ddiochel, ddiochwyth hawl,
Llywelyn heilyn, hwylfeirdd waddawl,
Llawenydd i ddydd, i ddeddf ai mawl,
Llewychedig llafn yn llaw reddfawl,
Yn lladd, dy wrthladd iwrth lys *Rheidiawl*,
Gweleis a gerais ni gar mantawl,
Gwelygordd *Lleiſſion* llyſſoedd gweddawl,
Lluoedd arwoloedd ar weilw didawl,

R   Llawrwyr

Llawrwyr am eryr yn ymeiriawl,
Llywelyn lleyn, llyw ardderchawl,
Lluriglas, gwanas, gwanau a hawl,
Gwenwyn yn amwyn am dir breiniawl *Powys*,
Ae diffwys, ae glwys a glyw ei hawl,
Ef dynniad ynghad, *Eingl* frad freuawl,
Ef dandde rhuddle *Rhuddlan* is gwawl,
Gweleis *Lywelyn*, eurddyn urddawl,
Yn urddas dreigwas dragywyddawl,
Eil gweleis i dreis dros ganol *Dyfrdwy*,
Yn y trei tramwy llanw rhwy, rhwydd hawl
Gweleis aer am gaer oedd engiriawl,
Talu pwyth dydd gwyth, canyseawl,
Ni rywcleis neb na bo canmawl,
O'r ddau y gorau a fo gwrawl.

Mi ath arwyre, ath arwyrein myfyr,
Eryr yn rhywyr, prifwyr *Prydein*.
Prydfawr *Lywelyn* pryd dyn dadiein,
Prydus, diefcus, efcar ddilein.
Efcynnu ar llu ar lle *Ewein*,
Yfgymmod gorfod, gorfalch am brein,
Yfgymmyn gwerlyn, gwerlid gofiein,
Yfgymydd clodrydd, *Kulwydd* a *Llwyfein*,
Lluddedig edmyg, meirch mawrthig mein;
A lluoedd yngwifcoedd yn ymofcrein,
Ar llinyn ar dynn ar du cclein,
A llinon rhag Bron rhag bro *Eurgein*,
Tyrfa *Clawdd Offa* clod yn hofficin,
A thorfoedd *Gwynedd* a gwyr *Llundein*,

Cyfran

Cyfran tonn a glan, glafdir gwylein,
Golud mowr yftrud, yfgryd *Norddmein*,
Llywelyn terwyn, torf anghyngein,
Biau'r gwyr goreu, bachau bychein,
Priodawr mwynglawr *Mon* glod yfcein,
Areul golud pentud, *Pentir Gwychein.*
Gwawr *Debau* gorau, gwyr yn dyrein,
Gwenwyn a gwanar y ddau gar gein,
Ae lyw cyferyw, cyfwyrein a thrin,
A thrychieid gwerin *Caer Fyrddin* fein,
Ni fefis na thwr, na bwr, bu crein,
Nag argoed, na choed, na chadlys drein,
A rhag pyrth bu fyrth *Saefon* ynghrein.
Oedd trift maer, oedd claer cleddyf heb wein,
A chan llu pannu, pen ar ddigrein,
A chan llaw lludwaw *Llan Huadein,*
Cil Geran achlan, a chlod goelfein,
A chlwyr ar dyhedd, mawredd mirein,
Yn *Aber Teifi* tew oedd frein uch benn,
Yn yd oedd perchen parchus gyfrein.
Oedd tew peleidr creu, creuynt gigfrein,
Calanedd gorwedd gorddyfnaffein,
Llywelyn boed hyn boed hwy ddichwein,
No *Llywarch* hybarch, hybar gigwein.
Nid celadwy dreig, dragon gyngein,
Nid calan cyman gwr y gymein,
Hydwf yngnif ai lif o lein,
Hyd ydd el yn rhyfel hyd yn *Rhufein,*
Ai raglod ai rod o riw Feddgein,
Hyd i dwyre haul hyd y dwyrein.

R 2

Ys imi rwydd Arglwydd, argleidrad,
Argledr tir, a gwir a gwenwlad,
Ys imi or cyngor cyngwafdad,
Cywefti peri peleidrad,
Ys imi ri ryfel ddiffreiddiad,
Diffryd gwyr, eryr ardwyad,
Ys imi rwydd Arglwydd, erglywiad
A glywir o'r tir gar *Tanad*,
Ys imi glew, a llew a lleiddiad
Yn rhyfel a rhon orddyfniad,
Ys imi wr a wared i rad,
I reidus, galarus, geilwad.
Ys imi ner yn arwyn ddillad,
Yn arwein yfgin yfgarlad,
Ys imi *Nudd*, hael fudd, Hueil feiddiad,
Ar *Lloegr* ryllygrwys heb wad.
Ys imi *Rydderch*, roddiad aur melyn,
Molitor ymhob gwlad.
A mawrdud olud olygad,
A *Mordaf* am alaf eiliad,
Ys imi *Run* gatcun gytcam rad,
Cydgaffael, a hael, a hwyliad
Ef imi y meddwl difrad,
Mi iddaw yn llaw yn llygad,
Ni henyw o afryw afrad,
Mi hanwyf o henwyr ei dad,
Llachar far, aerfar, erfynniad,
Llachar fron o frydau *Gwriad*.
Lluchieint gweilch am walch gynnifiad,
Fal lluchynt eftrawn wynt *Tylrad*.

4   Hunydd

Hunydd nen perchen parchus fad,
Parch arfawr, *Arfon* angoriad.
Llywelyn dreis, erlyn drwfliad,
Dros *Dehau* angeu oth angad,
Angor mor y mawr gymynad,
Angawr llawr llurig Duw am danad.

Rhy chyngein *Prydein* yn ddibryder,
I Briodawr llawr yn llawn nifer.
Llywelyn gelyn yn i galwer
I gelwir am dir am dud tymer.
Llawenydd lluoedd llew ymhryder,
Llywiawdr ymmerawdr mor a lleufer,
I ddylif cynnif cynhebyccer
I ddylann am lann, am leifiaid ffer.
Terfyfc tonn ddilyfc ddyleinw aber :
Dylad anwafdad ni ofteccer.
Terwynt twrf rhywynt yn rhyw amfer,
A rhialluoedd lluoedd llawer.
Torfoedd ynghyhoedd ynghlyflawnder
Tariannau golau mal i gweler:
Ry folant anant, anaw cymer,
Ry molir i wir i orober,
I wryd yn rhyd yn rheid nifer,
I orofn gwraf yn ydd eler,
I orfod gorfod glod a glywer,
I wyr am eryr ni amharer,
I warae orau pan waräer,
I wayw a orau yn ddau hanner,

Dinidr

Dinidr yn nyddr brwyd yn yd brofer,
Dinoding perging, pargoch hydrfer,
Dinas, dreig urddas, eurddawn haelder
Dinag o fynag pan ofynner,
Dyn yw *Llywelyn* llywiawdr tyner,
Doeth coeth cywrennin, gwin a gwencr,
A'r gwr ai rhoddes ni ran o'r pader,
Ai rhoddo ef gwenfro gwynfryn uch fer,

A R W Y R A I N

V.

ARWYRAIN

Owain Gwynedd. Gwalchmai ai cant.

ARDDWYREAF hael o hil *Rodri,*
  Ardwyad gorwlad, gwerlin teithi,
Teithiawg *Prydain,* twyth arfdwyth *Owain,*
Teyrnain ni grain, ni grawn rëi.
Teir lleng i daethant, liant leftri,
Teir praff prif lynges wy bres brofi,
Un o'r *Iwerddon,* arall arfogion
Or *Llychlynigion,* llwrw hirion lli.
Ar drydedd dros for o *Norddmandi,*
Ar drafferth anferth, anfad iddi.
A dreig *Mon* mor ddrud i eiffillyd yn aer,
A bu terfyfc taer i haer holi,
A rhagddaw rhewys dwys dyfyfci,
A rhewin a thrin a thranc Cymri,
A'r gad gad greudde, a'r gryd gryd graendde,
Ac am dal *Moelfre* mil fannieri,

5

A'r

A'r ladd ladd lachar, ar bar beri,
A ffwyr ffwyr ffyrfgawdd ar fawdd foddi,
A *Menai* heb drai o drallanw gwaedryar,
A lliw gwyar gwyr yn heli :
A llurygawr glas, a gloes trychni,
A thrychion yn nhud rhag rheiddrudd ri,
A dygyfor *Lloegr*, a dygyfranc a hi,
Ag ei dygyfwrw yn aftrufi,
A dygyfod clod cleddyf difri,
Yn faith ugain iaith wy faith foli.

A W D L

VI.

A   W   D   L

A gant Einiawn fab Gwalchmai, i Neſt ferch Hywel.

AMSER Mai maith ddydd, neud rhydd rhoddi,
  Neud coed nad ceithiw, ceinlliw celli,.
Neud llafar adar, neud gwar gweilgi,
Neud gwaeddgreg gwaneg, gwynt yn edwi,
Neud arfeu doniau, goddau gwedi,
Neud argel dawel·nid meu dewi,
Endewcis i wenyg o Wynnofi dir,.
  I am derfyn mawr meibion *Beli*,.
Oedd hydreidd wychr llyr yn llenwi,
Oedd hydr am ddylan gwynfan genddi,
Hyll nid oedd ei deddf hi hwyreddf holi,
Hallt oedd i dagrau, digrawn heli,
Ar helw bun araf uch bannieri ton,
  Tynhegl a gerddais i gorddwfr *Teifi*,.
Ceintum gerdd i *Neſt* cyn noi threngi,
Cânt cant i moliant mal *Elifri*,
Canaf gan feddwl awrddwl erddi,
Caniad i marwnad, mawr drueni !
    S   Canwyll

Canwyll *Cadfan* lan o lenn bali.
Canneid i fynnieid gar *Dyfynni*,
Gwan, wargan, wyrygall, ddeall ddogni,
Gwreig nid oedd un frad gariad genthi,
Gweryd rhudd ai cudd gwedi tewi,
Gwael neuedd maenwedd mynwent iddi,
Golo *Nef* goleu ddireidi.
Golwg gwalch dwythfalch o brif deithi,
Gwenned gwawn ai dawn oi daioni,
Gwynedd anrhydedd, oedd rhaid wrthi,
Nid oedd ffawd rhy gnawd rhin y genthi,
Gnawd oedd dâl eur mal er i moli,
Ni ryfu dognach er i dogni poen,
  Penyd a fo mwy no'r meu hebddi,
Neum gorau angau anghyfnerthi,
Nid ymglyw dyn byw o'r byd fal mi,
Ni chyfeirch angen iawlwen ioli,
Er neb rhy barther i rhyborthi,
Nef yn ei haddawd, wenwawd weini,
Ydd wyf pryderus fal pryderi.
Pryderwawd ceudawd, cyfnerthi ni wnn,
  Nid parabl yw hwn ni fo peri.
Llen argel iffel y fy'm poeni,
Lludd *Gwen* lliw arien ar *Eryri*.
Archaf im Arglwydd culwydd celi,
Nid ef a archaf arch egregi,
Arch, ydd wyf un arch yn i erchi,
Am archfein riein, reid y meini,
Trwy ddiwyd eiriawl deddfawl *Dewi*,
A deg cymmeint feint fenedd *Frefi*,

          Am

Am fun a undydd i hammodi,
A'r gyſtlwn pryffwn y prophwydi,
Ar gyfoeth Duw doeth i detholi,
Ar anghyweir *Meir* a'r merthyri,
Ag yn i goddau gweddi a ddodaf,
      Am dodeis nwyf im addoedi.
Ni bu ddyn mor gu gennyf a hi
Ni bo poen odder, *Pedr* wy noddi,
Ni bydd da gan Dduw i diddoli,
Ni bo diddawl *Neſt*, nef boed eiddi.

VII.

Llywarch Brydydd y Moch ai cant,

I Lywelyn fab Jorwerth.

CRIST Greawdr, llywiawdr llu daear a nef
  Am noddwy rhag afar,
Crist celi, bwyf celfydd a gwar,
Cyn diwedd gyfyngwedd gyfar.
  Crist fab Duw am rhydd arllafar,
I foli fy rhwyf rhwyfg o ddyar,
Crist fab Mair am pair o'r pedwar defnydd,
  Dofn awen ddiarchar.
Llywelyn llyw *Prydain* ai phâr,
Llew a glew a glyw gyfarwar,
Fab Jorwerth ein cannerth an car,
Fab Owain ffrawddicin, ffrwyth cynnar,
  Ef dyfu dreig llu yn llafar ddillat,
  Yn ddillyn cyfarpar,
Yn erfid, yn arfod abar,
Yn arfau bu cenau cynnar,
Yn ddlengmlwydd hylwydd hylafar
Yn ddidranc ci gyfranc ai gar,
Yn *Aber Conwy*, cyn daffar fy llyw,
  Llywelyn athrugar,
A *Dafydd*, defawd *Ul Caiffar*,

           Difai

Difai ddraig, ddragon adwyar,
Difwlch uddd difalch i efgar,
Difwng blwng blaen ufel trwy far,
Dybryd in feirdd byd bod dacar arnaw,
   Ac arnam i alar.
Ef yn llyw cyn llid gyfyfcar,
Yfglyfion yfglyfiynt llwrw bar,
Oedd rynn rudd ebyr or gwyr gwar,
Oedd ran feirw fwyaf o'r drydar,
Oedd amliw tonnau, twnn amhar eu neid,
   Neud oeddynt dilafar.
Ton heli ehelaeth i bar,
Ton arall guall, goch gwyar.
Porth Aethwy pan aetham ni ar feirch mordwy,
   Uch mowrdwrf tonniar,
Oedd ongyr, oedd engir ei bar,
Oedd angudd godrudd gwaedryar,
Oedd enghyrth ein hynt, oedd angar,
Oedd ing, oedd angau anghymar,
Oedd ammau ir byd bod abar o honam,
   O henaint lleithiar.
Mawr gadau, anghau anghlaear,
Meirw fengi, mal feri fathar,
Cyn plygu *Rodri*, rwydd efgar, ym *Mon*
   Mynwennoedd bu braenar,
Pan orfu pen llu llachar,
Llywelyn llyw *Alun* athafar,
Myrdd bu lladd, llith brein gorddyar,
O'r milwyr, a mil yngharchar.
Llywelyn cyd lladdwy trwy far,

2

Cyd llofgwy, nid llefg ufeliar,
Llary deyrn, uch cyrn cyfarwar
Llwrw cydfod ir clod is claiar,
Ry llofies rwyf treis tros fanniar i feirdd,
Oedd fawrllwyth ir ddaear,
Gwifci aur ag ariant nis car.
Gwafewynfeirch goffeirch, gofathar,
Yfginfawr gorfawr, gorwymp par,
Yfcarlad lliw ffleimiad, fflamiar,
Meirch Mawrthig, ffrwythig, ffraeth, anwar,
Ffrawddus, a phreiddiau ewiar.
Mwth i rhydd, arwydd yngwafcar,
Mal *Arthur* cein fodur cibddar,
Cann a chann, a chein wyllt a gwar,
Cant a chant a chynt nog adar.

Adar weinidawg, caeawg Cynran drud,
Dreig *Prydein* pedryddan,
Addod *Lhegr*, lluoffawg am bann,
Addaf hir in herwydd calan,
Adwedd teyrnedd tir nis rhan,
A dan fer ys fef i amcan,
Adnes i franhes i frein bann,
Dychre dychrein gwyr ynghreulan,
Gwrdd i gwnaeth uch Deudraeth *Dryfan*,
Gwr hydwf, gwrhydri *Ogyrfan*
Dygwydd gwyr heb lafar heb lan,
Dygoch llawr dwygad fawr faran,
Un am fro *Alun*, elfydd can,

A *Ffrainc*

A *Ffrainc* yn ffrawddus ma! *Camlan* ;
Ar eil yn *Arfon* ar forfan,
Yn undydd an un Duw in a ran,
A dwy dreig ffeleig, ffaw gymman
Mal deulew ein dylochaffan,
Ag un traws gatcun, treis faran,
Fal gwr yn gorfod ymhobman,
Llywelyn llafn-eur anghyfan,
Lloegr ddiwrcidd, llu rhuddfleidd *Rhuddlan*,
Llu rhagddaw a llaw ar llumman,
Llwybr yn wybr yn ebrwydd allan,
Llwrw ddawn *Cadwallawn fab Cadfan.*
I mae am *Brydain* yn gyfan,
Llary ni ddel ei law ettaw attan,
Llyried tra myned tramor dylan,
Rhag llaith anolaith anolo llan,
A llafnawr lledrudd uch grudd a gran,
Ninnau Feirdd *Prydein,* prydus eirian berth,
      Gwyr a byrth fy rhwyf ymhob calan,
Er digabl barabl gan bawb oi fan,
Digrifwch elwch elyf egwan,
Oi ariant gormant gorym ni drudran,
O'i alaf ai aur ai ariant can.

Gan i ddwyn dychryn a ddechreuo bleid,
      Uch blaenwel yn oed llo,
Gnaws achaws yn ych cyn adfo,
Gnawd i ladd ni lwydd i abo.
Caer Lleon llyw *Mon* mwyn *Pabo* ath dug,
Ef ath dwg ynghodo,

Llywelyn

Llywelyn ef llofges dy fro,
Llas dy wyr dra llyr, dra llwyfo,
Llwyr dug y *Wyddgrug*, nid ffug ffo,
Llœgrwys i llugfryd i fynnio,
Llewdir teyrn lluddiwyd yn agro,
Llas i glas, i glwyftei neud glo,
Llys *Elfmer*, bu ffêr, bu ffwyrngno,
Llwyr llofged i thudwed ai tho,
Llwrw gwelwch neud heddwch heno
Gan fy rhwyf, nid rhyfedd cyd bo,
Hyd i del i dorf ar dyno a bryn,
Udd breiniawg bieufo,
Llew ai dug, ai dwg pan fynno,
Ir *Trallwng* trillu anwofgo,
Llys efnys, afneued tra fo.
Lles i fyrdd o feirdd ai cyrcho.
Addug y *Wyddgrug* ai dycco, . .
Gwyliwch gwylyddwr, pwy ai lluddio,
Llwrw *Fochnant* edrywant ar dro,
Llwytewn llwyth llithiwyd am honno,
Lletcynt *Argœdwys*, gwys greudo,
Llys a dwy neud einym ni heno.
Edryched *Powys* pwy fo,
Brenin breifg werin, brwyfg agdo,
Ai gwellygio pwyll rhydwyllo :
Ai gwell *Ffranc* no ffrawddus *Gymro.*
Llyw y fy ym, fynniwch cyd tawo,
Lloegr gychwyn, a fynn a fynno,
Llwyr i dyd i fryd ar fro *Gadwallawn*
Fab Cadfan, fab Iago,

Llary

Llary yfpar ys penyd iblo,
Llwrw efpyd yfpeid anolo,
Llew prydfawr llyw *Prydain* ai chlo,
Llywelyn lliaws ei fran fro,
Llary deyrn cedyrn, cad wofgc; ynghur
  Ys fy nghar a orffo.

Gorfydd Udd dremrudd, dramor lliant,
Ym *Môn Mam Gymru* bedryddant,
Gorllwybr llu llenwis ewyngant,
Gwarthaf bryn a phenrhyn a phant,
Gorllanw gwaed am draed a ymdrychant,
Amdrychion pan ymdrechaffant,
Cad y *Coed Anau*, Cadr anant borthi,
  Burthiaift wyr yn nifant.
Ail gad trom i tremynaffant,
Udd addien uch *Dygen Ddyfnant*,
Eil miloedd mal gwyr dybuant,
Eil yrth gyrth in gwrthfynnaffant,
Eil agwrdd ymwrdd am hardd amgant bre
Bron yr Erw i galwant,
Cynwan llu fal llew yth welfant,
Cadr eryr ith wyr yn warant,
Can hynny cynhennu ni wnant,
Can wyllon *Celyddon* cerddant.
Dugoft y *Wyddgrug*, a dygant i dreis
  Adryffedd cyfnofant,
A *Rhuddlan* yn rhuddliw amgant,
Rhun can clawdd adrawdd edrywant.

     T   A *Dinbych*

A *Dinbych* wrthrych gorthorrant ar fil,
    Ar *Foelas* a *Gronant*
A *chaer yn Arfon*, a charant yngnif,
    Yngnaws coll am peiriant,
A *Dinas Emreis* a ymrygant,
Amrygyr ni wneir na wnant
Neur orfydd dy orofyn nad ant
Ith erbyn ith erbarch feddiant
Neu'r orfuwyd yn orenw *Morgant*
Ar filwyr *Prydain* pedryddant
Dy gynnygn ni gennyw cwddant,
Ni gaiff hoen na hun ar amrant,
Mad ymddugoft waed, mad yth want,
Arall yn arfoll yfgarant,
A chleddyf, a chlodfawr yth wnant,
Ag yfgwyd ar yfgwydd anchwant,
Mad tywyflaifd dy lu, *Loegr* irdant,
Ar derfyn *Mechain* a *Mochnant*,
Mad yth ymddug dy fam, wyd doeth,
Wyd dinam, wyd didawl o bob chwant,
O borffor o bryffwn fliant,
O bali ag aur ag ariant, .
O emys gochwys gochanant dy feirdd,
    Yn fyrddoedd i caffant.
Minnau om rhadau rhymfuant,
Yn rhuddaur yn rhwydd ardduniant:
O bob rhif im Rhwyf im doniant,
O bob rhyw im rhodded yn gant
Cyd archwyf im llyw y lloergant yn rhodd,
Ef am rhydd yn geugant.

Lliwelydd lledawdd dy foliant,
Llywelyn, a *Llywarch* rwy cant.
Munerawd ym marw fy mwyniant fal yn byw
  Lleiffiawn ryw *Run* blant.
Nyd gormod fy ngair it gormant!
Teyrn wyd tebyg *Eliphant*,
Can orfod pob rhod yn rhamant,
Can folawd a thafawd a thant.
Cein deyrn, cyn bych yngreifiant,
Can difwyn o yfgwn efgarant,
Can Dduw ren yn ran weftifiant
Can ddiwedd pob buchedd, bych fant.·

VIII.

L L Y M A

B U M A W D L

A gant Llygad Gwr, i Lywelyn fab Gruffudd.

I.

CYFARCHAF i Dduw, ddawn orfoledd,
  Cynnechreu doniau, dinam fawredd,
Cynnyddu canu, can nid rhyfedd dreth,
    O draethawd gyfannedd,
I foli fy Rhi rhwyf *Arllechwedd*,
Rhuddfäawg freiniawg o frenhinedd,
Rhyfyg udd *Caiſſar*, treis far troſſedd,
Rhuthrlym, grym *Gruffydd* etifedd,
Rhwyfyſg frwyfg, freifg, o freint a dewredd,
Rhudd barau o beri cochwedd,
Rhyw iddaw diriaw eraill diredd,
Rhwydd galon, golofn teyrnedd.
Nid wyf wr gwaglaw wrth y gogledd,
O Arglwydd gwladlwydd, glod edryſſedd,
Nid newidiaf naf un awrwedd a neb,
    Anebrwydd dangnefedd.

                                    Llyw

Llyw y fy ym ys aml anrhydedd,
Lloegr ddifa o ddifefl fonedd,
Llywelyn gelyn, galon dachwedd,
Llary wledig gwynfydig *Gwynedd,*
Llofrudd brwydr, *Brydein* gywryfledd,
Llawhir falch, gwreiddfalch gorfedd,
Llary, hylwydd, hael Arglwydd eurgledd,
Llew *Cemmais,* llym dreis drachywedd,
Lle bo cad fragad, friwgoch ryfledd,
Llwyr orborth hyborth heb gymwedd,
Gnaws mawrdraws am ardal dyhedd,
Gnawd iddaw dreiddiaw drwyddi berfedd,
Am i wir bydd dir or diwedd,
Amgylch *Dyganwy* mwyfwy i medd,
A chiliaw rhagddaw a chalanedd creu,
Ag odduch gwadneu gwaed ar ddarwedd.
Dreig *Arfon* arfod wythlonedd
Dragon diheufeirch heirddfeirch harddedd,
Ni chaiff *Sais* i drais y droedfedd oi fro,
Nid oes o *Gymro* i Gymrodedd.

II.

Cymmrodedd fy llyw lluoedd beri,
Nid oes rwyf eirioes, aer dyfyfgi,
Cymro yw haelryw o hil *Beli* hir,
    Yn herwydd i brofi.
Eurfudd ni oludd, olud roddi,
Aerfleidd arwreidd o *Eryri,*

Eryr ar geinwyr gamwri dinam,
    Neud einym i foli.
Eurgorf torf tyroedd olofci,
Argae gryd, Greidiawl wrhydri,
Arwr bar, taerfar, yn torri cadau,
    Cadarnfrwydr yftofi.
Aer dalmithyr, hylithr haelioni,
Arf lluoedd eurwifgoedd wifgi
Arwymp Ner, hyder, hyd *Teifi* feddiant,
    Ni faidd neb i gofpi.
Llywelyn Lloegrwys feiftroli,
Llyw breiniawl, brenhinedd teithi,
Llary deyrn cedyrn, yn cadw gwefti cyrdd,
    Cerddorion gyflochi.
Coelfcin brein *Bryneich* gyfogi,
Cclennig branes, berthles borthi,
Ciliaw ni orug er caledi gawr,
    Gwr eofn ynghyni.
Parawd fydd meddiant medd Beirdd im Rhi,
Pob cymman darogan derfi,
O *Bwlffordd* ofgordd yfgwyd gochi hydr,
    Hyd eithaf *Cydweli.*
Can gaffael yn dda dra heb drengi,
Gan fab Duw didwyll gymmodi,
Ys bo i ddiwedd ddawn berchi ar nef,
    Ar neillaw Crift Gcli.

                                        Llyw

III.

Llyw y fy'n fynhwyrfawr riydd,
Lliwgoch i lafnawr, aefawr ufwydd,
Lliw deifniawg, llidiawg, lledled fydd ei blas,
    Llwyr waeth yw ei gas noi garennydd.
Llywelyn gelyn, galofydd,
Llwyrgyrch darogan cymman celfydd,
Ni thyccia rhybudd hael rebydd rhagddaw,
    Llaw drallaw drin wychyed.
Y gwr ai rhoddes yn rhwyf dedwydd,
Ar *Wynedd* arwynawl drefydd,
Ai cadarnhao, ced hylwydd yn hir,
I amddeffyn tir rhag torf ofwydd.
Nid aniw, nid anhoff gynnydd,
Neud enwawg farchawg, feirch gorewydd,
I fod yn hynod hynefydd *Gymro*,
A'r *Gymry* a'u helfydd.
Ef difeiaf Naf rhy wnaeth Dofydd,
Yn y byd o bedwar defnydd,
Ef gorcu riau reg ofydd a wnn,
Eryr *Snawtwn* aer gyfludwydd.
    Cad a wnaeth, cadarn ymgerydd,
Am gyfoeth, am Gefn Gelorwydd,
Ni bu gad, hwyliad hefelydd gyfred,
Er pan fu weithred waith *Arderydd.*
    Breifclew *Mon,* mwynfawr *Wyndodydd,*
Bryn *Derwyn* clo byddin clodrydd,

Ni bu edifar y dydd i cyrchawdd,
Cyrch ehofn eſſillydd.
Gwelais wawr ar wyr lluoſſydd,
Fal gwr yn gwrthladd cywilydd,
A welei *Lywelyn*, lawenydd dragon,
Ynghymyſc *Arfon* ac *Eiddionydd*,
Nid oedd hawdd llew aerflawdd llüydd,
I dreiſiaw gar Drws Daufynydd,
Nis plygodd Mab Dyn bu doniawg ffydd,
Nis plycco Mab Duw yn dragywydd.

IV.

Terfyſc taerllew glew, glod ganhymdaith,
Twrf torredwynt mawr uch mor diffaith,
Taleithawg deifniawg dyfniaith *Aberffraw*,
Terwyn anrheithiaw, rhuthar anolaith.
Tylwyth, ffrwyth, ffraethlym eu mawrwaith,
Teilwng blwng, blaengar fal goddaith,
Taleithawg arfawg aerbeirh *Dinefwr*,
Teilu hyſgwr, yſgwfl anrhaith.
Telediw gad gywiw gyfiaith,
Toledo balch a bylchlafn eurwaith,
Taleithawg *Mathrafal*, maith yw dy derfyn,
Arglwydd *Lywelyn*, lyw pedeiriaith,
Sefis yn rhyfel, dymgel daith,
Rhag eſtrawn genedl, gwyn anghyfiaith,
Sefid Brenin nef, breiniawl gyfraith,
Gan curwawr aerbeir y teir talcith.

4

Cyfarchaf

V.

Cyfarchaf i Dduw o ddechrau moliant,
    Mal i gallwyf orau,
Clodfori o'r gwyr a geiriau
I'm pen, y pennaf a giglau,
Cynnwrf tân, lluch faran llechau,
Cyfnewid newydd las ferau,
Cyfarf wyf a rhwyf, rhudd lafnau yngnif,
    Cyfoethawg gynnif cynflaen cadau.
Llywelyn nid llefg ddefodau,
Llwybr ehang, ehofn fydd mau,
Llyw yw hyd *Gernyw* aed garnedd i feirch,
    Lliaws ai cyfeirch, cyfaill nid gau,
Llew *Gwynedd* gwynfeith ardalau,
Llywiawdr pobl, *Powys* ar *Dehau,*
Llwyrwys caer, yn aer, yn arfau,
Lloegr breiddiaw am brudd anrheithiau,
Yn rhyfel, ffrwythlawn, dawn diammau,
Yn lladd yn llofci yn torri tyrau,
Yn *Rhos* a *Phenfro,* yn rhysfäau *Ffrainc,*
Llwyddedig i ainc yn llüyddau.
Hil *Gruffudd,* grymmus gynneddfau,
Hael gyngor, gyngyd wrth gerddau,
Hylathr i yfgwyd, efcud barau gwrdd,
    Hylym yn cyhwrdd cyhoedd waedffau.
Hylwrw fwrw far, gymmell trethau,
Hawlwr gwlad arall gwledig riau,

           U   Harddedd

Harddedd o fonedd, faen gaerau dreifddwyn,
Hirbell fal *Fflamddwyn* i fflamgyrchau.
Hwylfawr ddreig, ddragon cyfeddau,
Heirdd i feirdd ynghylch ei fyrddau,
Hylithr i gwelais ddydd golau i fudd,
        Ai feddgyrn wirodau.
Iddaw i gynnal cleddyfal clau,
Mal *Arthur* wayw dur i derfynau,
Gwir frenin *Cymru* cymmreifc ddoniau,
Gwrawl hawl boed hwyl o ddehau.

L L Y M A

IX.

L L Y M A

O D L A U'R M I S O E D D,

A gant Gwilym Ddu o Arfon, i fyr Gruffudd Llwyd o Dref-garnedd a Dinorweg yn Arfon; allan or Llyfr Coch o Hergeft, yngholeg yr Iefu yn Rhyd Ychen.

NEUD cyn nechrau Mai mau anrhydedd,
    Neud aeth yfgwaeth a maeth a medd,
Neud cynhebyg, ddig, ddygn adroffedd drift,
Er pan ddelid Crift, weddw athrift wedd!
Neud cur a lafur im wylofedd,
Neud cerydd Dofydd, nad rhydd rhuddgledd.
Neud cof fy ynnof, ys anwedd e faint,
Neud cywala haint, hynt diryfedd.
Neud caeth im dilyd llid llaweredd,
Neud caith Beirdd cyfiaith am eu cyfedd.
Neud caethiwed ced, nad rhydd cydwedd *Nudd*,
Cadrwalch *Ruffudd*, brudd, breiddin tachwedd,
Neud cwyn Beirdd trylwyn, meddw ancwyn medd,
Neud cawdd im anawdd, meneftr canwledd,
Neud carchar anwar enwiredd Eingl-dud,

U 2   Acrddraig

Aerddraig *Llan Rhyftud* funud fonedd.
Neud nim dyhudd budd, bum arygledd,
Neud nam dilyd llid, lliaws blynedd.
Neud nam dawr, Duw mawr, maranedd, Ne fglyw,
Neud nad rhydd fy llyw, llew *Trefgarnedd*,
Neud trwm oi eifiau dau digyfedd.
Neu'r wyr Beirdd canwlad, nad rhad rheufedd,
Neud ef arwydd gwir, neud oferedd gwyr,
Wrth weled f' eryr yn ei fowredd;
Neud truan im gwân gwayw lledfrydedd,
Neud trwydded galed im amgeledd.
Neud trymfryd *Gwynedd*, gwander dyedd braw :
Neud hwy eu treifiaw am eu troffedd.
Neud trahir gohir gloyw babir gledd,
Oedd trablwng echwng *Achel* ddewredd.
Neud trai cwbl or Mai, mawredd allwynin,
Neud Mis Mehefin weddw orllin wedd.
    Neud Mis Mehefin, mau hefyd gyftudd,
Neud nam rhydd *Gruffudd* wayw rhudd yn rhyd.
Neum rhywan im gwân gwayw cryd engiriawl,
Neud am Ddraig urddawl didawl im dyd.
Neum erwyr om gwyr im gweryd Crift Ner,
Neud arfer ofer, Beirdd nifer byd.
Neud arwydd nam llwydd lledfryd im calon,
Neud eres nad tonn honn ar ei hyd.
Mau ynnof mowrgof am ergyd gofal,
Am attal arial *Uren* yngryd.
Mal cofain cywrain *Cyweryd*, fardd *Dunawd*,
Meu im Dreig priawd gwawd ni bo gwyd.
Mau gwawdgan *Afan*, ufuddfryd ffrwythlawn,

    4   O gof

O gof *Gadwallawn*, brenhinddawn bryd.

Ni wn waith gwaywdwn, gwawd ddihewyd clod,

A thi heb ddyfod pa dda bod byd?

Neud wyr pawb yn llwyr, lleyrfryd gynnat,

Nad hylithr aur mâl mal oddiwrthyd.

Nid oes nerth madferth ym myd, oth eifiau,

Gwleddau na byrddau na Beirdd ynghlyd.

Nid oes lys yfbys, efbyd neud dibeirch,

Nad oes meirch na feirch na ferch hyfryd.

Nad oes wedd na moes, maffw ynyd yw'n gwlad,

Nad oes mad eithr gwad a gwyd.

Neud gwagedd troffedd, traws gadernyd *Môn*,

Neud gweigion *Arfon* is *Reon* ryd.

Neud gwann *Wynedd* fann, fenn ydd ergyd cur,

Neud gwael am fodur eglur oglyd.

Neud blwyddyn i ddyn ddiofryd a gar,

Neud blaengar carchar, grym aerbar gryd.

Gwilym Ddu o Arfon ai cant, yn y Flwyddyn 1322.

L L Y M A

X.

L L Y M A

D D Y H U D D I A N T   E L P H I N.

I.

E LPHIN deg taw ath wylo
    Na chabled neb yr eiddo
Ni wna les drwg-obeithio
Ni wyl dyn ddim ai portho
Ni fydd goeg gweddi *Cynllo*
Ni thyrr Duw ar addawo:
Ni chad yngored *Wyddno*,
Erioed cyſtal a heno.

II.

Elphin deg fych dy ddeurudd
Ni weryd bod yn rhy brudd
Cyt tybiaiſt na chefaiſt fudd
Nith wna da gormod cyſtudd
Nag ammau wyrthiau Dofydd
Cyt bwyf bychan wyf gelfydd,
O foroedd ag o fynydd
Ag o eigion afonydd
I daw Duw a da i ddedwydd.

III.

Elphin gynneddfau diddan
Anfilwraidd yw d' amcan
Nid rhaid yt ddirfawr gwynfan
Gwell Duw na drwg ddarogan
Cyd bwyf eiddil a bychan
Ar fin gorferw mor dylan
Mi a wnaf yn nydd cyfrdan
Y't well no thrychan maran.

IV.

Elphin gynneddfau hynod
Na forr ar dy gyfaelod
Cyt bwyf gwan ar lawr fy nghod
Mae rhinwedd ar fy nhafod
Tra fwyf fi yth gyfragod
Nid rhaid yt ddirfawr ofnod
Drwy goffau enwau'r Drindod
Ni ddichon neb dy orfod.

TALIESIN ai dywawd.

It may not be improper to inform the Reader, that the ORTHOGRA-
PHY *ufed in thefe Poems is the* ORTHOGRAPHY *of the* MSS.
and not that of the WELSH BIBLE.

D I W E D D.

A P P E N D I X,

N°. I.

A METHOD how to retrieve the ancient Britiſh language, in order that the Bards of the ſixth century may be underſtood,
and that the genuineneſs of Tyffilio's Britiſh Hiſtory, which was
tranſlated from the Armoric language into Latin by Galfridus Arturius
of Monmouth may be decided; and concerning a new edition of
Gildas Nennius's Eulogium Brittanniæ, with notes, from ancient Britiſh MSS. This old Britiſh writer has been ſhamefully mangled by
Dr. Gale, his editor, in the Scriptores Britannici; and not much
mended by Mr. Bertram in his late edition of it at Copenhagen.

WHETHER the ancient Britiſh language can be ſo far recovered as
to underſtand the moſt ancient Britiſh writings now extant, is, I think,
a conſideration by no means beneath the notice of a ſociety of Antiquarians, and of all learned men in general. There has been, it is
true, an attempt of this nature made by the very learned Mr. Edward
Llwyd, of the Muſeum, and in part laudably executed in his Archæologia Britannica, which reflects honour on thoſe worthy perſons who

X   ſupported

fupported him in his five years travels into Ireland, Scotland, Cornwal, Baffe Bretagne, and Wales. But as his plan was too extenfive to bring every branch of what he undertook to perfection, I think a continuation of the fame, reftrained within certain limits, might ftill be ufeful.—Natural hiftory is itfelf a province fufficient to engrofs a man's whole attention; but it was only a part of this great man's undertaking: and the learned world is abundantly convinced of the uncommon proficiency he made in natural philofophy; and how induftrious he was in tracing the dialects of the ancient Celtic language. But ftill it muft be acknowledged that he did very little towards the thorough underftanding the ancient Britifh Bards and hiftorians. And indeed he owns himfelf that he was not encouraged in this part of his intended work, as appears by his propofals. Far be it from me to cenfure thofe very learned men who generoufly contributed to fupport the ingenious author in his travels, and dictated to him the method he was to purfue. But, after all, I cannot help lamenting that he did not pay more attention to the old MSS. and compile a gloffary to underftand them. What he has done of this nature is very imperfect, few words being added to what there are in Dr. Davies's dictionary, and thofe chiefly from writings of the fourteenth and fifteenth century. Indeed it appears he had not feen the works but of one of the Bards of the fixth century, and that in the red book of Hegeft, in the Archives of Jefus's College, Oxon. He complains he could not procure accefs to the collections at Hengwrt and Llan Fordaf, and without perufing thofe venerable remains, and leifure to collate them with other copies, it was impoffible for him to do any thing effectual.—Now the method I would propofe to a perfon that would carry this project into execution, is, that as foon as he is become mafter of the ancient Britifh language, as far as it

can be learned, by the affiftance of Dr. Davies's dictionary, and
Mofes Williams's gloffary at the end of Dr. Wotton's tranflation of
Howel Dda's laws, he fhould endeavour to procure accefs to the great
collections of ancient Britifh MSS. in the libraries of the Earl of
Macclesfield, Lady Wynne of Wynftay, the Duke of Ancafter, Sir
Roger Moftyn at Gloddaith, John Davies, Efquire, at Llannerch,
Mifs Wynne of Bod Yfcallen, Wiliam Vaughan, Efquire, at Corfy
Gedol, and in other places both in South and North Wales in private hands. By this means he would be enabled in time to afcer-
tain the true reading in many MSS. that have been altered and
mangled by the ignorance of tranfcribers. I am fatisfied there are
not many copies of the Bards of the fixth century extant, nor indeed
of thofe from the conqueft to the death of Llywelyn. But two or
three ancient copies on vellom, if fuch can be met with, will be fufficient; for in fome tranfcripts by good hands that I have feen, they
are imperfect in fome copies. This would in a great meafure enable
our traveller to fill up the blanks, and help him to underftand what,
for want of this, muft remain obfcure, if not altogether unintelligi-
ble. We fhould by the means of fuch a perfon have a great many
monuments of genius brought to light, that are now mouldering
away with age, and a great many paffages in hiftory illuftrated and
confirmed that are now dark and dubious. Whole poems of great
length and merit might be retrieved, not inferior, perhaps, to Offian's
productions, if indeed thofe extraordinary poems are of fo ancient
date, as his tranflator avers them to be. The Gododin of Aneurin
Gwawdrydd is a noble heroic poem. So are likewife the works of
Llywarch Hen about his battles with the Saxons, in which he loft
twenty-four fons, who all were diftinguifhed for their bravery with
golden torques's. *Aurdorchogion.*

TALIESIN's poems to Maelgwn Gwynedd, to Elphin ap Gwyddno, to Gwynn ap Nudd, and Urien Reged, and other great perfonages of his time are great curiofities. We have, befides thefe, fome remains of the works of Merddin ap Morfryn, to his patron Gwenddolau ap Ceidis, and of Afan Ferddig to Cadwallon ap Cadfan; and, perhaps, there may be in thofe collections fome befides that we have not heard of. All thefe treafures might be brought to light, by a perfon well qualified for the undertaking, properly recommended by men of character and learning: and I think, in an age wherein all parts of literature are cultivated, it would be a pity to lofe the few remaining monuments now left of the ancient Britifh Bards, fome of which are by their very antiquity become venerable. Aneurin Gwawdrydd above-mentioned is faid, by Mr. Robert Vaughan of Hengwrt, to be brother to Gildas ap Caw, author of the Epiftle de *excidio Britanniæ*, which is the moft ancient account of Great Britain extant in Latin by a native.—No manner of eftimate can be made of the works of our Bards and Hiftorians that have been deftroyed from time to time; nay fome very curious ones have been loft within this century and a half. I think, therefore, it would be an act becoming the Antiquarian Society, and all patrons of learnning in general, to encourage and fupport fuch an undertaking, which would redound much to their honour, and be a fund of a rational and inftructive amufement.—Nor would thofe benefits alone accrue from a thorough knowledge of our Bards, but ftill more folid and fubftantial ones. For who would be better qualified than fuch a perfon to decide the controverfy about the genuinenefs of the Britifh Hiftory, by Tyfilio, from the oldeft copies of it now extant, which differ in a great many particulars from the Latin tranflation

of

of Gulfrid, who owns that he received his copy from a perfon who brought it from Armorica ; and why may there not be fome copies of it ftill behind in fome monafteries of that country, and of other works ftill more valuable ? Mr. Llwyd, of the Mufeum, intended to vifit them all, in order to get a cata.ogue of them to be printed in his Archæologia Britannica ; but he was prevented by the war which then broke out, of which he gives an account in a letter to Mr. Rowlands, author of Mona Antiqua reftaurata, and which is publifhed at the end of that treatife. Who can be better qualified to fucceed in fuch an undertaking than a perfon that is thoroughly well verfed in all the old MSS. now extant in Wales. I find that the Armoric hiftorians, particularly Father Lobineau, quote fome of their ancient Bards to confirm hiftorical facts. This is demonftration that fome of their oldeft Bards are ftill extant; and who knows but that fome of the books they took with them when they firft went to fettle in Gaul, under Maximus and Conau Meiriadoc, may be ftill extant, at leaft tranfcripts of fome of them ; for that fome were carried over is plain, by what Gildas himfelf fays, " quæ vel fi qua fuerint, aut ignibus " hoftium exufta, aut civium exulum claffe longius deportata non " compareant." So that I would have our traveller pafs two years at leaft in Baffe Bretagne, in order to make enquiry after fuch ancient monuments, and I make no doubt but he would make great difco-veries.—Thus furnifhed, he might proceed to the Britifh Mufeum, the Bodleian library, and the library of the two Univerfities, and elfewhere, where any ancient Britifh MSS. are preferved. We might then have better editions of Britifh authors than we have had from the Englifh antiquaries, though in other refpects very learned men ; but, being unacquainted with our language, Bards, and antiquities, they have nothing but bare conjectures, and fome fcraps from the

Roman

Roman writers to produce. No one likewife would be better qualified to fix the ancient Roman ftations in Britain, as they are fet down
in Antoninus's intinerary, and their ancient Britifh names. — I wifh
learned men would think of this ere it be too late; for one century
makes a great havock of old MSS. efpecially fuch as are in the
hands of private perfons, who underftand not their true value, or
are fuffered to rot in fuch librarics, where nobody is permitted to have
accefs to them.

A P P E N D I X,

A P P E N D I X,

Nᵒ. II.

Infert after Sir John Wynne of Gwydir's account of the dif-
perfion and maffacre of the Bards, in the introduction
to the ode infcribed to Sir John Gruffudd Llwyd, p. 45.
the following addition :

IT is taken from an old Britifh grammar, written in Englifh, by
Wiliam Salefbury, printed at London, 1567. I have tranfcribed
it faithfully according to the old orthography. "Howbeit when
" the whole Ifle was commonlye called Brytayne, the dwellers
" Brytons, and accordingly their languuage Brytifhe, I will not refell
" nor greatly deny ; neither can I juftly gainfaye, but their tongue
" then was as copious of fyt woordes, and all manner of proper
" vocables, and as well adornated with woorfhipful fciences and ho-
" nourable knowledge as any other of the barbarous tongues were.
" And fo ftill continued (though their fceptre declined, and their
" kingdom decayed, and they alfo by God's hand were driven into
" the moft unfertyl region, bareneft country, and moft defart pro-
" vince of all the ifle) untyll the conqueft of Wales. For then, as
" they fay, the nobles and the greateft men beyng captives and brought
" pryfoners to the tower of London, there to remayne during their
" lyves,

" lyves, defired of a common requeft, that they might have with
" them all fuch bokes of their tongue as they moft delited in, and
" fo their petition was heard, and for the lightnefs foon granted,
" and thus brought with them all the principalleft and chiefeft
" books, as well of their own as of other their friends, of whom
" they could obtain anye to ferve for their purpofe. Whofe mynde
" was none other but to pafs the time, and their predeftinate perpe-
" tual captivitie in the amenous varietie of over reading and revo-
" luting many volumes and fundry books of divers fciences and .
" ftrange matters."

" And that is the common anfwer of the Welfhe Bardes (for fo
" they call their country poets) when a man fhall object or caft in
" their teeth the foolyfh uncertainty and the phantafticall vanities
" of their prophecies (which they call BRUTS) or the doubtful
" race and kinde of their uncanonized fayndtes : whom that not-
" withftanding they both invocate and worfhip wyth the moft hyghe
" honoure and lowlieft reverence. Adding and allegyng in excufe
" thereof, that the reliques and refidue of the books and monuments,
" as well as the fayndtes lyves, as of their Brutyfh prophecies and
" other fciences (which perifhed not in the tower, for there, they fay,
" certain were burned) at the commotion of OWAIN GLYNDWR,
" were in like manner deftroyed, and utterly devaftat, or at the leaft
" wyfe that there efcaped not one, that was not uncurablye maymed,
" and irrecuperably torn and mangled.

> " Llyfrau Cymru au llofrudd
> " Ir twr Gwyn aethantar gudd
> " Yfceler oedd Yfcolan
> " Fwrw'r twrr ly frau ir tan.

              Gutto'r Glyn.   A. D. 1450.

                          " The

" THE books of Cymru and their remains went to the White
" Tower, where they were hid. Curfed was Yfgolan's act in.
" throwing them in heaps into the fire."

THE Author living at a diftance, from the Prefs, the following
infcriptions of two of the Odes were by miftake omitted in their
proper places:

ODE II. Page 14.

To Mifs WILLIAMS of PENIARTH, on the Banks of DYSYNNI,
this ODE is infcribed by her

Moft Obedient

Humble Servant,

EVAN EVANS,

ODE VI. Page 27.

To Mifs PUGH, of COETMOR, the following POEM is infcribed
by her

Moft obedient

Humble Servant,

EVAN EVANS.

Y   To

To the Note about Sir Gruffudd Llwyd, Page 48, *add:*

" Edward Philipp Pugh, Efq; of Coetmor, in Carnarvonfhire, is
" a defcendant in a direct line from Ednyfed Fychan, and has in
" his cuftody a grant from prince Llywelyn the Great of fome lands
" in Creuddyn given to the faid Ednyfed, and his pofterity, with the
" prince's feal in green wax affixed to it. To this worthy gentle-
" man, and his lady, I am much obliged for their civility when I
" lived in thofe parts.—The royal family of the Tudors are likewife
" defcended from Ednyfed Fychan, as appears by a commiffion that
" was fent to the Bards and Heralds of Wales, to enquire into the
" pedigree of **Owain Tudor**, king **Henry** the **Seventh's** grand-
" father."

F I N I S.

ADDENDA ET CORRIGENDA.